HOMETOWN HEARTACHE

M. J. Schiller

CHAPTER ONE

Nash

I came to New York City, like so many others, to find fame and fortune. Or at least fame. But, like so many others, instead of taking a bite out of the Big Apple, it took a bite out of me. I showed my portfolio at any number of studios, and while they all seemed impressed, no one was willing to give me a chance. "It's the damned economy," they'd tell me. "We're not taking any chances on newcomers. Sorry."

So, on to Plan B.

Plan B included spending much too much of my inheritance on a small studio of my own, in Upper Manhattan, until I could build my reputation enough for others to become interested in me. But even Plan B had its drawbacks. While the poor economy should have made buying into the real estate market a piece of cake, we were still talking NYC, where property was always at a premium. But, determined to see this thing out until it came to its natural death, I continued to look for the perfect place to hang up my canvases and get down to the work of making a name for myself in the art community, if only as an unrelenting nuisance.

Uncomfortable as I was with big city realtors, I put away my apprehension and pushed my way through the revolving doors of a swank hotel, making my way to the five-star restaurant inside. As I walked toward the table the maitre de indicated, I began to have a surreal feeling, like time was coming to a jarring stop. Ahead of me, a woman, dressed in business attire, sat way too close to a man whose voice I recognized from my phone calls, Jack Duran, major New York realtor. Though the woman was turned away from me, seeming to be rapturously absorbed by whatever Jack was saying to her, an oddly-placed sense of familiarity came over me.

Jack glanced up as I neared the table. "Hello, Jack." I reached out to shake his hand. The woman turned slowly to look up at me, a smile still on her face, and my heart skipped a beat.

"Nash!" She literally jumped in her seat as if I had struck her.

"You two know each other?" Jack asked, displaying an innate grasp of the obvious.

Chloe peered at me for a second, then she flashed her gaze back to Jack, seeming at a loss for words. She looked wonderful—her full lips dressed in a rich scarlet, her hair, unmanageable at times when we were growing up, had, through some mysterious adult female trick, become luxuriously full and soft-looking. She was as stunning as she was the first day I met her, when her hair was done up in braids and she was boasting an Annie Oakley cowgirl out-fit, complete with tasseled, white boots and a white felt hat, set askew by un-even pigtails. But somehow it always came down to those fantastic eyes of hers, which seemed to reach in and grab hold of your heart, as if she'd lassoed them with the rope forever slung at her hip back in those cowgirl days.

"It's good to see you, Chloe," I said roughly, my voice catching a little on her name. I held out my hand.

She slipped her—I couldn't help but notice—well-manicured hand daintily into mine. "Yes, um, Nash. Good to see you, too," she replied, tripping over her words like a circus clown climbing into the ring. I slid into the booth across from her, taking in the deep fuchsia, silk blouse, unbuttoned far enough to offer up the tantalizing curves of her bosom, and the snug, little black blazer she wore on top of it, sharply cut to accent that shapely figure as well. She stared at me, her mouth agape, for several seconds—her beautiful eyes wide, but unread-able—then dropped her gaze to the table cloth, focusing intently on the dark-ening ring her sweating glass of ice water left.

I half-listened to Jack as he rambled on about some property or other, but my eyes kept drifting expectantly to Chloe, unable to believe, after all these years, that she sat across from me, our knees close to touching under the table, my heart racing away, with me hanging on for dear life. How many pictures in my portfolio were of her? Nudes, profiles, and just vibrant, swirling colors which represented the confused emotions she often brought out in me... I gave my attention briefly to Jack.

"...is in your price-range, but it needs a little work..."

I nodded, trying to appear engaged, before again sliding my gaze to Chloe. This time, as I looked, her gaze flitted up to mine and held for a second. I was surprised to see tears in her eyes, and utter disbelief and confusion. She glanced down again and her tremulous hand reached for the water glass. She took a sip, and then seemed to center herself, because the next time she raised her eyes, they were smiling falsely, appearing distant and disconnected, as if she had turned off a switch deep inside her. And I was amazed by how seemingly effortless it was for her; she didn't show an ounce of emotion throughout the rest of the meal. I got the feeling this detachment was much more the standard for her; the brief bit of genuine feeling I glimpsed in her was what was a rarity, as far as Chloe Carmichael went, that is.

I wished it were as easy for me. My insides were a tangled up heap of mismatched socks. I was both excited and terrified, love-sick and car-sick, my stomach lolling about like a puppy in freshly mown grass. I barely ate a bite of my fifteen-dollar steak sandwich.

"So... How do you two know each other?" Jack asked, filling up the awkward silence I accidentally let descend on the table, intent as I was on trying to calm my nerves while still basking in Chloe's nearness. The realtor was unable to keep the hint of jealous suspicion out of his voice. He looked from me to Chloe, licking his lips.

She spoke up, as if having been prodded with a stick. "Oh. We grew up together. Yes, Nash is an old family friend." She said the last with a trace of bitterness on her sweet tongue. Neither of us elaborated further, but even Jack could read the tension between us like storm clouds rolling in to block the morning sun.

By the time the meal was over, I agreed to see any number of properties the following afternoon, hoping to put an end to the painful conversation as soon as possible, wanting to get Chloe alone. I excused myself finally, making up some lame story about a lawyer's appointment, and left. I chanced a glance back as I left the room, wishing to catch those breathtaking green eyes again, but Chloe only stared blindly at her water glass, while Jack examined her with a frown.

Outside, I paid a valet attendant to let me park my truck near the front, so I could see her come out. Minutes later, the pair strolled through the door, Jack seeming miffed and Chloe obviously trying to reassure him. As I watched, she reached up on her tiptoes and pulled his head down to whisper in his ear. He laughed and slid his arms around her, letting his hands move down to grab her ass, tightly housed, I saw now, in a short black skirt. My eyes wandered, as his hands had, over her firm rear and the seeming endlessness of her legs, lengthened even more by the racy black heels she wore. They cut a pretty picture—Chloe, light and sensual, Jack, tall, broad-chested, with dark blond, well-groomed hair and a glowing smile. My hands gripped the steering wheel, observing until the valet maneuvered a sleek, red Ferrari into the spot in front of the hotel where the awning and red carpet ended. Jack reached to open the door for her. She folded her long legs into the vehicle, laughing, head tilted flirtatiously as her eyes danced over the high-priced realtor.

An unfamiliar tightening in my chest grabbed me, and I fought to swallow the fire which seemed to be rising within me, choking me with its intensity. I automatically steered my beat-up, blue pickup truck onto the street behind the red Ferrari, following it through the thick knots of traffic in the downtown theatre district. I could see through the rear window she was sitting nearly on top of him.

Don't those things have stick shifts, for God's sake?

As we pulled up at the next light, his arm was around her and she was kissing his neck. Then, in horror, I watched her disappear completely. In his rearview mirror, his eyes widened in pleasure. I witnessed his struggle as he tried to concentrate on the road in front of him and had to, in fact, squeal to a stop at a pedestrian crosswalk, barely in time to miss an angry, gray-haired Oriental woman who flipped him the bird. Chloe's head reappeared after that, and they seemed to get a good laugh out of it before continuing on.

By the time the fancy sports car pulled up in front of a modest, brick-fronted condominium on the west side near Central Park, I was fuming. Mad at him, mad at her, and most of all, mad at myself for caring. Jack came around to Chloe's side of the car and reached in to help her out. Those legs poured themselves out of the car and onto the sidewalk, and I looked on irately as the giggling pair vanished into the heart of the building. I parked, and waited.

Chloe

I was flirting with Jack. He was an okay guy, good-looking, in his own way, and loaded. Man, was he loaded. I didn't really like him at all. I simply liked to make men want me. Not that I was a tease, mind you; they never left unsatisfied. I was good at it. It was the one area where I excelled. But it was always a very "no strings attached" kind of relationship, and they usually liked it that way. They didn't even have to please me. I would please them, so I kept the upper hand.

Then Nash walks right in and plops down in the booth across from me. My stomach fell away like that time at the State Fair on the Tom Twister, when the floor dropped out from under me leaving me stuck to the wall by centrifugal force. But even in that memory, Nash was there. I couldn't remember a time when he wasn't, except for when he wasn't for good, when he went away to school.

When I looked up to see him standing by the table, I was swamped by that feeling again, the feeling of abandonment which overwhelmed me when he'd left a swirling void of nothingness in my life. He hadn't changed much in all the time since we'd last met, those cute freckles were gone, but he still had an open face and his general boyish good looks. His brown hair was, perhaps, a little thinner, but still rich and glossy; his jawline seemed maybe a tad sharper and stronger. Those expressive brown eyes, which were as homey as mud-pies, could still draw me in and make me feel warm all over.

But when all I'd had left was the memory of those eyes, I was filled with a deep chill instead. And now, seeing him once more, I froze for a moment. Then I dug deep and pulled myself together. I was surprised. I never would have thought I would be capable of knitting up that hole with him sitting right there, breathing in the same air as me.

Of course it created an even stronger urge in me to do Jack. If I had Jack, literally, by the balls, I could feel like I had a hold on my life, like it wasn't about to smash into a thousand brilliant pieces. If I had Jack, willing to do about anything for me to reach that rushing escape, then I didn't need to be scared. I was in charge. And I could close my eyes to the fact the world I created was little more than a crystal bubble, and Nash was the hammer who could smash it to bits.

CHAPTER TWO

Nash

I sat in my car, the early spring sun making me over-warm despite the cool air surrounding me. Growling at no one in particular, I slid my hands along the steering wheel in opposite directions, and then back again. I alternated between staring straight ahead at the back end of an old Buick, and glancing up at the doorway, asking myself why I was there. Why was it so important for me to speak to Chloe Carmichael? I mean, obviously she'd moved on with her life. Obviously she wasn't lying awake at night imagining me beside her. Why beat myself up? But Chloe had stolen my heart long ago, and I had a right to take it back from her, and to give her my two cents worth in the process, and then some.

I looked up again as a little girl was about to pass my car. She had on a white, frilly dress and was licking at a partially-melted chocolate ice cream cone, which had dripped down her front and comically ringed her mouth. She wore pigtails with white yarn tied around them, and I couldn't help but think of the first day I met Chloe.

It was a warm, early spring day, like today...

I watched from my bedroom window, peering through the branches of the huge oak tree growing at the corner of the front of the house. A large moving van backed slowly up the long, rambling gravel driveway. I held my breath, and repeated in a low whisper, "Please have a boy my age. Please have a boy my age."

When the truck finally came to a stop, and the door of the cab opened, a cowboy hat appeared on someone about my size and I whooped with glee, pounding down the stairs and out the back door, slamming the screen door as I hollered over my shoulder, "They have a boy! They have a boy!"

My mom called after me as she iced a chocolate cake. "Nash Steven Nabry, you get back here this instant. The last thing they need is you underfoot."

But I ignored her, running pell-mell to the truck, kicking up rock behind me. Even now I can recall the scratch of my tennis shoes as I made a sliding stop in front of her, scattering gravel left and right, and the way the rock dust filled my throat and nostrils as much as my indignation. "You're a girl," I spat.

"Nash!" my mother's appalled voice yelled from several yards behind me. I still don't understand how she could always hear every impolite word I spoke, yet not hear me when I called up the stairs asking her where the cereal was. Then Chloe's father came around the back end of the truck, and the grownups introduced themselves while I stared at Chloe and Chloe stared at me like this was a showdown at the O.K. Corral, which was fitting considering her outfit. Looking back, my mind automatically added the dramatic, high-pitched, whistling notes from the theme song to *The Good, the Bad, and the Ugly*, a Clint Eastwood movie my brother, Ed, liked to watch. Chloe rubbed a fist in her eye, which probably was irritated by the chalky, drifting dust I raised from the gravel, squinting the other eye in the bright sunshine as she glared at me.

I remember my bitter disappointment like it was yesterday. A girl. Why did it have to be a girl? The only boys to play with in the area were my two older brothers, and they were merciless to me, my being the baby and all.

"Nash!" my mom called to me exasperatedly. I looked up. I got the feeling she had been talking to me for some time. "Why don't you go show Chloe here the creek?"

"But, Mom..." I started to whine. The glare I got in return brought me up short. She meant business. I turned from my mother and frowned at Chloe for a second. "Well, come on then." I took off up the driveway, marching as fast as I could, hoping to get it over with. Once out of earshot, I turned and asked sarcastically, "Can't ya keep up?"

She stared at me wordlessly, and I could have sworn she dragged her feet even more as we proceeded. She was a pain in the butt then, and undoubtedly a pain in the butt now. After a while, she abandoned her little project of irritating me and ran to keep up, apparently excited about the prospect of a creek in her back yard.

"What's with the cowgirl outfit?" I asked, begrudgingly admiring the faux-mother-of-pearl buttons down the front and what, I considered at the time to be, real spurs on her heels.

"I dunno," she returned with a shrug. "I guess I just like it." She wrinkled her nose up in that cute way she had and smiled at me.

For the first time, I felt the stirring in my heart which was patently Chloe Carmichael. I slid my gaze her way from time-to-time as we walked. She was kind of pretty, with a splash of freckles across her cheeks and the bridge of her nose, long, auburn hair, with copper highlights I could now see as her hat slipped off to hang down her back by its string. She had these phenomenal, heart-shattering eyes, the exact color of my favorite cat's-eye marble.

The scent of damp earth and mossy rock carried to us on the wind as we neared the creek. "That yours?" she asked, nodding in the direction of my abandoned bike.

I nodded, thinking quickly. "I left it here this morning when I was jumping the creek," I lied, trying to appear casual. My brothers had jumped the creek, but I never had. I had almost worked up my nerve to do it earlier that morning, but my mom called me in to clean my room.

"You can jump that?" she asked doubtfully, scanning the expanse of the creek, probably a good five feet in the spot we stood in front of.

"Sure," I boasted. "I do it all the time. Watch." I ran up and righted my fire-engine red bike, grabbing on to the high handle bars and climbing on the white banana seat which only had one patch of silver duct tape on it at the time. I walked it backward, angling it toward the huge dirt mound my brothers erected so they could get some air over the creek. You have to understand, Evil Knevil was big in those days. As I grasped the handle bars, I moved my hands front and back, acting like I was revving up a motor, and making the appropriate accompanying sounds. Chloe smiled at me, and, I swear, in that second, I felt like I could hop three creeks side-by-side. I got a good start, the multi-colored plastic ribbons on the grips of my handle bars streaming behind me boldly. I hit the ramp, flew up into the air...and plowed into the opposite bank dead on, wedging my front wheel in the mud and the crossbar in my gut. I slid off with a splash into the water.

Chloe screamed and waded out to me. "Are you okay, Nash? Are you okay?"

"I'm fine," I croaked bravely, wrapping my arm around my middle as if I could protect it post-jump.

I must have looked pretty bad, because Chloe was very upset. "Your lips are gray. Can you breathe? I think I should get your mom."

"No, don't!" I cried out, forcing breath through my battered lungs. "She'd kill me if she found out I tried to jump the creek."

A slow smile crossed her face. "I thought you said you'd done this before."

"I have," I stammered, coming up with a cover story. "It's just...she doesn't know about it." I could tell Chloe wasn't buying it.

"Okay." She gave my arm a soft, reassuring touch, sending my heart into orbit. "But you're sure you're okay?"

"Ahh," I bluffed, though still grimacing. "I'm fine. Oh, geez. Look at your boots."

She looked down at her muddy boots and laughed. "It's all right. I've got another pair. And besides, I get them muddy all the time."

I grinned up at her, sitting on the mud-slick bank with my hands wrapped around me, suddenly happy as a clam the new neighbor was a girl.

I wore a mirror image of that grin as I thought about it behind the steering wheel years later, staring blindly at the Buick in front of me. I shook myself and glanced around, catching the reflection of my eyes in the rearview mirror.

Then I thought about spying Jack Duran's eyes in the rearview mirror as Chloe did—whatever it was she was doing—to him, and all the good feelings drifted away.

Chloe

I let Jack kiss me. I was even less into it than I usually was. All I could think about was Nash.

Jack insisted on taking my keys and opening the door himself. He liked to be in control. That's alright. Let him think that. He'd be putty in my hands in a few minutes. Without holding the door for me he marched in, leaving it open behind him. I exhaled. Quite the gentleman.

"This place is a sty." He picked up my Yankees cap from off the couch and threw it in the chair, like that really helped. He threw his legs in the air and plopped down, taking the hat's place and clonking his shoes down on my coffee table. I tilted my head and tsk-tsked in my head.

"Yeah. I know. I was running late this morning," I lied. I collected a dirty glass, plucked the sections of the newspaper from the coffee table, folding them and tucking them under my arm before grabbing the ball cap.

"Get me a drink, would ya, hon?"

I forced my jaw to relax. "Of course."

He picked up a magazine and began flipping through the pages, not giving any page more than a cursory glance. I took my junk into the kitchen, set the hat on the counter and the glass in the sink, then stuck the paper in recyclables. I got a tumbler down for Jack, clinked some ice in it, and poured the scotch. As

I turned, I accidentally knocked the hat off the counter. When I bent to pick it up, I was struck by a memory.

It was a fall day, when we were about eleven. Nash and I were traipsing along the creek bed, me dragging a stick in the mud behind me lazily, thinking the path it made was like Hansel and Gretel's trail of bread crumbs, leading us home. I was wearing denim shorts and one of those baseball T-shirts, white down the middle with a navy collar and sleeves, a Mets symbol adorning one pocket. Conversely, I had my hair threaded through the Yankees baseball hat. My loyalties could be bought cheap in those days. Nash had on one of his favorite T-shirts, and one I loved, too. It was navy, with a picture of the Fisher Price Little People Mom on the front, only she didn't have on her usual sunny smile. She had her cliché plastic hairdo all right, but the face was changed to an angry face and the words underneath said, "If Momma ain't happy, ain't nobody happy."

We'd spent the morning collecting buckeyes for our thriving business. Okay, so it wasn't exactly thriving, but one never knew when a run on buckeye necklaces might occur. We dropped them, with a clunk, into my metal Holly Hobbie lunchbox, and filled both Nash's Star Wars lunchbox, and mine, chock-full. But I had a strange feeling this enterprise may go south like our rock business had. With that undertaking we hauled wagons full of boulders from the creek bed. Hard, sweaty work, and we'd only sold a handful to members of Nash's family. Pity sales; the worst kind.

Despite his fatigue, Nash suddenly grabbed my hand and helped me up the steep embankment, my well-worn Keds sliding through the mud and dried-up leaves.

"I want to show you something," he said excitedly, leading me into a wooded area we had never explored together before. He led me through the brush, since no trail existed. We hopped over fallen trees and scratched ourselves on branches, but we didn't care. Before long we had quite a collection of those flat little bur things on our socks. But the sun was shining, and the air smelled fresh, like leaves, piled high and glowing crimson, gold, and orange. We broke into a clearing, and it sprang up, a strange sight in the middle of nowhere. Around a stout tree trunk, a large, square platform was built with a half-wall around the edges. An iron-rod ladder ascended mysteriously into its core.

"Wow," I breathed. "Whose is this?"

"Ours," he said cockily, dragging me over to the ladder and scrambling up.

"I don't know. Do you think we should?" I glanced around the empty clearing with uncertainty. "What if the real owners show up?"

He stuck his head down with a huge grin. "Come on up, you big baby."

"Shut up," I countered, but I was grinning. I had no choice but to follow him. He'd thrown out the ultimate challenge and called me a baby. The only thing worse would have been if he'd stuck his hands under his armpits, flapped his "wings" and called me a chicken.

When I stuck my head through the hole in the floor, he was leaning, his hands flat on the ledge where the walls met, looking out as if inspecting his kingdom.

"Isn't this great?"

"Yeah." I walked around inside, trailing my hand along the massive tree's trunk. The fort was completely empty, and its only decoration seemed to be the green, rubbery outdoor carpeting secured to the bottom, and a big, rusty-red felt rooster nailed to one of the sides. "What's with the rooster?"

He shrugged. "I dunno." Not one to let such a minor detail perturb him he flopped down with a contented sigh, bunching up his jacket for a pillow. I untied mine from my waist and lay next to him. We gazed at the clouds drifting lazily past in silence.

It was like the voices echoed to me over the years, no matter how hard I tried to silence them. I ran my finger along the brim of the hat, feeling a smile quirk my lips. I didn't even remember picking it up, or setting down the glass in my hand.

Jack's voice thundered from the front room. "What the hell are you doing in there? Where's my drink?"

I grasped the counter with both hands and made a conscious effort to relax my jaw. If I didn't, my TMJ would act up. I took his glass and swigged down the scotch, then reached for the bottle to refill it.

"Coming!"

CHAPTER THREE

Nash

After an hour, Jack came out, tripping down Chloe's condo steps, practically whistling Dixie. I decided he was well-named because he definitely was an ass. I watched him leave and then, like I was on automatic-pilot, I stormed out of my truck, slamming the door and taking the stairs to her condo two at a time. An elderly woman was entering carrying groceries, and I snagged the door as it was shutting, scraping my fingers on the bricks as they became wedge in the small crack. Ignoring the pain, I muscled the door open and entered the foyer. With the loud roaring in my head, the hallway seemed strangely quiet, the old lady having disappeared down a short set of stairs. I peered at the mailboxes. Carmichael, C., 210B.

I rushed up the stairs, huffing by the time I reached the top, but not pausing before locating her door. I pounded on it so loudly a tenant down the hall opened his door. A skinny, Latino man wearing sagging jeans and a sleeveless undershirt peered at me, his thin mustache twitching, eyes hard.

I nodded at him. "Hey," I said roughly. He stared at me for a second, then turned around and closed his door. As soon as he was gone, I pounded again.

Chloe opened the door, a smile on her face, no doubt expecting Jack came back for more, but no man recovers that quickly. When she saw me, her jade green eyes turned as hard as the stone they looked like they were carved out of, and she clutched her black silk robe to her throat. Nice. Like she was going to hide from me what she'd let him see. "Nash, what are you—"

I pushed past her into the room, not wanting to hear her try to turn me away. "Nice place, Clo. Do you entertain all your men here?" Now that I was alone with her, my fury spilled out of me like poison, having become more venomous with each night I lay awake thinking of her, wishing she was beside me.

Her eyes narrowed. "You have no right—"

"No. Of course I don't." My mind reeled with the thought of them together in this room. Where had they been? On the couch? In the bed? On the floor? In the shower? Or had they just done it up against the wall? I came over to grab her by the hips and hauled her to me, my anger coursing through me. "But I thought I'd come up and see if I could score me some action, too, huh?" I nuzzled her ear roughly, but then was stung by the tantalizing smell of her skin. She fought me, trying to squirm out of my grasp. "Huh, Clo? What about me? Aren't you going to do me, too?"

"Stop it!" she screamed, pushing against my chest uselessly, her voice rising to near hysterics. "Let me go."

"Oh, come on, baby," I taunted meanly, feeling out of control. "I used to be good enough for you. Aren't I good enough for you anymore?"

"STOP!" she shrieked, tearing herself free, her robe loose, almost falling open. Her eyes flashed green fire at me for a second and then she stepped up and struck me, hard, across the face and the room fell silent. She stared at me in horror, then she broke down, sobbing, sliding onto the couch and bending herself in two, her hands covering her face, her back shaking violently with each wracking breath.

I cursed myself, saying out loud, my voice dripping with the remorse which had washed over me. "Come on, Clo. Don't do that."

"Get out." The words came out muffled and broken as she didn't look up.

I reached to touch her shoulder, and she drew back, shrinking into the corner of the couch, her head coming up as she eyed me warily. "Why did you come here?" she sobbed, the question sounding more like an accusation.

As I looked at her, my insides began to quake. Her soft hair was ruffled, but no less pretty, shining in the light from the windows. Her skin was creamy smooth, and her lips, though bearing no trace of her former lipstick, were still moist and compelling, and, what's worse, I knew what they could do to me, what they had done to me. I sat on the couch next to her. "I don't know," I answered gruffly. "I thought maybe you'd be happy to see me."

"Happy to see you?" Her voice rose, incredulous. "When you walk in here, and...all but accuse me of being a whore?"

I turned my self-loathing back on her. "Well it wasn't me on the floor of that Ferrari," I snapped, regretting it the instant I'd said it.

Her face, which was already flushed with anger, became a deeper red for an instant, but then the fire went out of her eyes and they became listless, making her look far older than her twenty-three years. "*Please*, just leave me alone." The empty, pleading quality of her voice ripped through me. I started to speak, to implore her to forgive me, but she interrupted, the words she uttered shaking like the last leaves on a tree in November. "P-please, go." The pained look on her face took all the fight out of me. I rose from the couch, wanting so badly to reach down and scoop her up into my arms. But that was no longer possible for me; she was no longer mine.

I left, closing the door behind me with a soft click and shuffling down the hall like an old man. I sagged under the weight of being incredibly tired and disheartened. This wasn't how I wanted things to be between us. Why did I act like such an ass? I berated myself endlessly as I stumped down the stairs and out to my car. I sat behind my wheel again. The only thing keeping me from laying my head on the steering wheel and bawling like a baby was my vague awareness of the others passing me by on the street.

Her face haunted me. The hollowness in those beautiful eyes echoed a memory of mine.

I saw them first, the people from the church, on her porch. I eyeballed them as I climbed off the bus, swinging my backpack. Chloe was still chattering away to Mary Ellen Murphy as she gathered her things, but it was one of those gorgeous days which called a boy outside to play, so I'd had grabbed my stuff several stops before ours, ready to hop off as soon as the little red stop sign arm extended from the side of the bus. Something about the way the women were sitting on the porch swing, then stood when the bus came into view, sent a shiver up my spine. When Chloe got off and caught sight of them, the smile faded from her face, too. She froze for a split-second with a look of terror, and then something compelled her forward. Curiosity perhaps. I trudged behind her, never taking my gaze from the two spinster ladies, who looked at Chloe compassionately as she drew nearer, confirming my fear something was very much wrong.

"Hello, Chloe, dear," one of them said slowly, as if talking to someone unstable, or someone about to become unstable.

The other, taller, skinnier one spoke more brusquely, "Your momma's inside now. She'll be needin' you, Miss Chloe." Although her face was set like stone, her gaze followed Chloe in sadly, as if she wished to spare her this somehow.

I squinted at them for a moment, but when they turned and looked at me, I hurried off toward my house, not wanting to know why they came. I only got a few feet before Chloe screamed. I never heard anyone scream like that, but I knew it was her, her voice as familiar as my own. The piercing wail, almost animal-like in its intensity, cut through the air, and my head snapped around. The two ghoulish ladies scurried inside, aware now something went wrong. They'd overestimated the ten-year-old girl; she could be of no help to her mother right now. The screen door slammed shut after the house swallowed them up, making me jump. I stood motionless, watching to see if the screen door would spit the old bitties back out, but nothing happened. I listened hard for any sign of Chloe, and could make out the sound of her softly weeping, along with her mother's incessant repetition of the word, "Why?"

I started to walk to Chloe's, but a hand rested on my shoulder. I whirled around, not having heard anyone approach, and looked up to see my mom standing next to me. She read the question on my face. "Mr. Carmichael was in an accident at work," she said. I wondered what sort of "accident" an accountant could get into, but later discovered one of his clients, who lost a fortune on the stock market, literally, shot the messenger.

I looked back at the house, understanding now. He was gone. The man who held Chloe on his shoulders, acting the part of the horse for his little cowgirl, the man who pushed her on the swing set for hours at a time, never tiring of listening to his little girl's sweet laughter, the man I looked up to, and admired, and thought of as a surrogate father, the man who sat on the porch swing, smooching his wife when he thought no one was watching—vanished, leaving behind two broken women.

A few days later, she was standing by her father's grave, ten years old, holding a bouquet of white roses, wearing a black, frilly dress. Her nose and eyes were red, but she was no longer weeping. She looked like some kind of horror show zombie, her eyes so zoned out and unresponsive it was like she had checked out completely.

A month passed, and I was weaving through the legs of adults trying to fill her house with forced gaiety, a paper plate heaped with fried chicken and nearly-sauceless mostaccioli in my hands. White crepe paper, honeycombed, wedding bells hung from the mantle where a few sympathy cards still sat because someone had forgotten to put them away. I started to push through the swinging door into the kitchen to find Chloe, who hadn't been back to school since her dad's death, when her mom's voice carried to me, pitched high in anger. "Why can't you just be happy for me, Chloe Marie?"

Chloe stood beyond her mom by the kitchen sink, wearing a white, frilly dress I was sure she felt uncomfortable in. "I've tried, Momma. I've tried," she cried, and then burst into tears, running down the hall to the left of the kitchen and slamming her bedroom door. Mrs. Carmichael, soon to become Mrs. Tate Rodgers, sat at the small, laminate kitchen table and cried, her head between her hands. I backed out of the room.

Fifteen minutes later, as I gnawed morosely on a chicken bone, Chloe's mom came out of the kitchen, a smile plastered on her face, and thanked every-one for the nice shower. A week later, she married Tate Rodgers in the back yard under an umbrella, as the rain pelted us and ran down the window where I could see Chloe's face peeking out from behind the curtains.

When I left her apartment, her eyes had the same dead look in them they had at her father's funeral. The same hollowness as the day her mom remarried. I thought at that time I would give anything not to see Chloe hurting like that anymore, and now it was me who caused her eyes to reflect such pain.

I looked up at the sky as the first fat raindrops began to fall. The beautiful day had turned ugly as I sat reminiscing. It suited my mood perfectly. I started the car and drove away.

CHAPTER FOUR

Chloe

I stood by my window, staring down at Nash's beat-up truck, willing him to come back. The sky finally melted into raindrops and he started the engine and drove away.

How many times can your world be shattered and put back together again before the pieces won't fit any more? The only person who was left who could hurt me was Nash, and I'll be damned if he hadn't just done it. Nash was the only one, the only one who cared for me, who I let my guard down with, and now, the way he'd looked at me...

I didn't want to think about it. Didn't want to think of him at all. But the trip down Memory Lane started up again, like some sick reel-to-reel projector jumping to life in my mind.

On the day of this memory we had been traversing the creek, wandering here and there, mostly out of sound-distance from my evil stepfather, who, unfortunately, was in the picture by then. We ended up at the tree house, again lying side-by-side to stare at the clouds.

He took my hand. "I didn't see you in school today."

I didn't comment, my throat suddenly tight.

"How come?" he asked softly, sitting on one elbow so he could gaze down into my face.

My palms sweated. I avoided looking him in the eyes.

Ever since my baby sister was stillborn, my mom suffered from bouts of depression. When my dad was alive, he could fight her out of it, mostly by making her take her pills. That's why we moved out to the country in the first place, to give Mom a change of scenery.

After he died, my mom closed up for a couple of weeks, sat alone in a dark room without making a sound. This depression seemed to have sent her spiraling downward, and she didn't have the gumption to get out of bed in the morning. She had wasted away to sharp angles, and seemed listless whenever I brought her a tray in. The only thing she appeared to like was when I read her those corny romance novels, the type where the girl always had violet eyes and the boy was stronger than Zeus and Muhammad Ali combined. I'd never met anyone with violet eyes, but if it made Mom happy, then I was all for it. It killed me to see her like that, remembering how beautiful and vibrant she was before my dad died.

But then, one day, friends from work showed up and forced her to go out. She met Tate that night, and brought him back to our house, weeks after my father was laid in the ground. She'd been drinking, she needed someone, and he was willing to fill the bill. Thus my nightmare began.

Those first few weeks Tate was on his best behavior, brought her flowers, took her to dinner, was polite and respectful to me, but I didn't like him from the start. I hoped and prayed I was wrong about him—maybe I hated him because he wasn't my father—but there was something in those steel grey eyes, or something missing, I was never quite sure which. But those eyes would shine brightly and intensely when they looked at me, seeming to belie his innocuous words.

My mom turned into someone I didn't know. She started wearing low-cut or tight-fitting clothes, drinking more, and having loud sex. At first she seemed a little embarrassed when Tate would grab her in front of me, or make comments about their sex life, but pretty soon it didn't seem to bother her nearly as much, though she would drink more often, and greater quantities. Two weeks to the day Mom brought Tate home, he announced he was "going to make an honest woman" out of her. Shortly after the wedding, Tate turned mean, finding fault with my mom constantly, especially when it came to the bedroom. Mom withdrew again, and this time for good. She was no longer getting out of bed; she'd given up. Tate was becoming increasingly demanding, wanting me home all the time, watching me in a creepy way, either complimenting me inappropriately, or putting me down.

I pushed those thoughts aside. Nash was waiting for an answer to why I wasn't in school. An answer I owed him.

"My mom was sick again. I had to stay home and take care of her."

"Ahh." He laid back and gave my hand a squeeze. He didn't ask any more questions, and that was the beauty of Nash Nabry. He seemed to know when to pry, and when to hold back. It made him an incredible friend. He was as intuitive as his mom.

Nash's mom always understood my need to escape with her son. After all, the windows were sometimes open, so she was well aware of my stepfather's tirades. One time she even stuck up to the old buzzard. I guess she'd had enough.

My stepdad chased me out of the house, threatening me, as he often did. The old coot never figured out how to keep things quiet. He had one volume setting, and that was blaringly loud. Not to mention the way our screen door sounded like a shotgun when I slammed it, and again seconds later when he stormed out after me. He was a big guy, 6-foot tall, about two-hundred-fifty pounds, I guess, with orangish hair that was sort of a cross between strawberry-blond and red, though thinning. He had one of those open faces which made you trust him, at first. But when he got mean, it was scary. Some women would have considered him handsome, charming even, but he was as mean as a startled snake.

Nash's mom came roaring out of their house as I ran around our old, rusty swing set, dodging my stepdad's big, club-like hands and trying to judge how drunk he was. If he was stumble-drunk, I could wear him out and he would forget everything when he sobered up. If he was only slur-angry-drunk, it was better to take my beating, because if he did catch me, it would be ten times worse. As I wove, watching his face and hands to get a feel for his state, he threw the swing at me and caught my hip before I could get totally out of the way. The hard plastic felt like a wrecking ball, but I didn't give him the satisfaction of crying out. Mrs. Nabry barreled down her back steps, red in the face, and with a baseball bat swung over one shoulder. I gaped, and was so surprised I forgot to duck, the swing hitting me squarely along my right jaw line this time.

"Tate Rogers!" she screamed. "If you so much as touch another hair on Chloe's head I'll hurry along the sorry death you're hell-bent on, I swear."

My stepdad leered at her in a way that made my stomach turn. I knew what he was thinking, and if Nash had known, he would have hastened the bastard's sorry death for sure. "Oh, come on, Evie," he coaxed, turning his attention from me for a minute. "I need to straighten Chloe here out a little bit on a few points." By that he meant he was going to beat me for running away when he fondled my ass. "But I'm a reasonable man," he spouted, his voice slyly sweet, "maybe you could give me a few parenting pointers." He sidled up to her and she stepped back, waving her bat. She was all of five-foot-two and pear-shaped, a total mom, out to cuddle or swat the world in turn.

"You watch your step there, Tate." She flounced her shoulder-length, curly, auburn hair, which was already turning a little grey, and stared him down.

"Ooh. I like a feisty woman." He made a move for the bat, and she dodged as the school bus's tires crunching on the gravel reached our ears. I had been carefully edging toward the door, hoping to reach my bedroom and lock myself in, but when he looked up at the sound of the tires, I froze, directly in his line of vision. He lunged, and I made it to the back door before he grabbed my hair.

"Awh!" I cried out, trying to pull it in to relieve the pain. But he gripped it tighter, until his fingers were scratching my scalp. He jerked my head back so he could get a good look at my terrified eyes, his flashing with sick excitement, his face inches from mine.

"I'm calling the cops!" Mrs. Nabry screamed, running into her house. She must have decided she couldn't bring herself to hit somebody with a bat. Even someone as mean as Tate Rodgers.

"I guess we'll have to take this inside, huh, Chloe?"

I knew what awaited me inside, so I desperately scrambled for a chance to escape. I had the angle on the door so I yanked it open, scoring both his crotch and his nose at the same time. He let go, howling in pain, and I took off running along the creek, knowing he wouldn't follow me, but I'd be locked out that night. It was a night like many other nights...only sometimes I didn't get away.

So, whenever I would show up to hang out with Nash, Mrs. Nabry understood and I loved her for it. She never made me feel uncomfortable when I came over wearing bruises, and she didn't ask a lot of questions, though she would sometimes take it up with my stepdad. She would even let Nash out of his chores sometimes if we wanted to spend time together.

And so the tree house became our place. My safe house. How I longed for a place I could feel safe now.

Nash

As I drove away from her place, I flipped the wipers on, but it was one of those rains which didn't really give you enough to wipe, and the screeching scrape of rubber on glass began to drive me insane, so I took turns turning the wipers off and on as I drove. Still, the rhythmic droning of the blades made me even more depressed, so I switched on the radio, scanning the stations for some decent music, up, down, up, down...but quickly turned it off again. I wasn't in the mood for music after all.

A car pulled up behind me and even with its windows closed I could hear the pounding of the bass. The music made another memory resurface.

We were fifteen, long before I worked up the nerve to kiss her, and my brother, Ed, was getting married to Sissy Crychek. Ed invited Chloe, who he called "Little Bits." I think he loved her from the start, too. Not in the way I did, but like the little sister he didn't have. He never tired of teasing her, sometimes making her mad, but then he'd wheedle her back into a good mood and all would be forgiven.

The day of the wedding, things were crazy at our house. My mom was trying to get dressed and, at the same time, keep her three buffoonish sons from tearing their rented tuxes as we horsed around in the living room. Since Ed was six years older than me, and had been out of the house for some time, and Ron was away at college, we didn't get much time together, and when we did, we seemed to fall into old patterns, especially when we were in the house where we grew up together, and roughhousing was second nature.

We reassured Mom for about the tenth time we would "knock it off" and went to the kitchen for a drink. Ed had turned off the tap after pouring a glass of water when we heard the shouting.

"What the hell...?" Ed slammed his glass on the counter and headed out the back door, flanked by Ronnie and me.

We could see Tate through the big kitchen window. He had Chloe by the arm and was shaking her furiously. "You think you can go whore around with the neighbor boys, Chloe? Well, you got another think coming."

"Please, Tate," she begged.

"Where'd you get this little trampy dress, huh?"

"I... s-sold my bike..."

"You what?" he roared.

"Please, Tate. I just want to go and see Ed and Sissy get married, then I'll come straight home, I prom—"

The rest of her statement was lost in a wail as Tate backhanded her and she went flying out of view. We could see him, presumably standing over her with his hands on his hips. "You ain't goin' anywhere, beautiful." The way he said it had the hair standing up on my arms.

Ed growled and rushed forward, Ronnie and me right on his heels. When we got to the back of their house, we could see in the screen door. Tate was on all fours over Chloe, pinning her wrists to the ground and looking at her fiercely. She had her head turned toward the door, but her eyes were squeezed shut.

Ed rushed up the few back steps in one leap, screaming, "GET THE HELL OFF HER!"

His cry surprised Tate. His mouth fell open and he looked a little afraid of Ed, who played football in college and was at least six-five, two-hundred-seventy five pounds. As big as he was, I had never really seen him angry, up until that day. I looked down into Chloe's face. She had opened her eyes and was staring at us in horror, seeming embarrassed to be seen like this, trapped on the floor by her stepfather. She looked so tiny, her small wrists in his big, meaty hands, her eyes wide.

"How I discipline my stepdaughter is none of your boys' business," Tate said, licking his lips.

Ed banged on the wood frame of the screen door and it shook so hard I thought it would come off its hinges. He was breathing hard. "You...get...away...from her, right now. Or I'm callin' the cops."

Tate released Chloe's wrists, sitting back on his haunches and holding his hands out. "Sure, sure. We were only wrastlin' around, weren't we, Chloe-girl?" he said the last menacingly, looking at her with meaning. Chloe didn't respond. Still staring her in the eyes intently, he rose to his feet. "Congratulations, there, Ed. I hear you got yourself a real looker."

Ed tore into the room. This time I think he did bust one of the hinges. "DON'T YOU TALK ABOUT HER THAT WAY! DON'T YOU EVER TALK ABOUT SISSY, AT ALL!"

Tate backed out of the room, his hands up, but a sly smile on his face. "Sure thing, Ed. Didn't mean no offense."

He disappeared and a second or two of complete silence hung in the air. Then Chloe started to shake violently. She brought her hands up to cover her face, crying without making a sound.

"Hey, Little Bits," Ed said tenderly, kneeling down on one knee by her side. "It's okay, now, sugar. Don't cry." He clumsily rubbed her arm. She flew up without warning and threw her arms around him, sobbing into his tux. Ed looked over at us helplessly.

Ronnie went and crouched by them. "Hey, Clo?" She lifted her head a little. "Do you want to come over to our house for a while?"

She took a deep breath, wiping the tears from her face. "No, no," she replied shakily. "It's Ed's wedding day. You don't need any of this..." She waved her hand vaguely, but seemed to run out of energy for her response.

"No, now," Ronnie continued, looking at me. "We want you to come over, don't we, Nash?" He nodded at me impatiently. I was still in shock.

I shook myself. "Yeah, Clo. Come on over. There's nobody my age around. I need you to balance things out."

She looked up at me, and started to smile. "Okay."

Ed helped her to her feet. "There, now. Nashie here didn't have any date, anyhow. You can be his date."

I glared at him, and Chloe blushed, not looking at me, seeming embarrassed by the notion. She looked down at her dress and gasped. "Oh. It ripped." Tate's pawing had created a jagged tear by her shoulder. It was clear she was crushed.

"Oh, that's no big thing," Ed reassured her quickly, no doubt worried about more tears falling. "Mom could have that fixed up in no time."

"Oh, but it's your wedding day. She probably has a million things to do. I couldn't—"

"Nah. You know Mom. She's had everything done for weeks and she's been driving us crazy all morning. Believe me, you'd be doing us," he gestured back and forth between the three of us, "a *big* favor if you keep her busy."

She smiled at him. "You're sure, Ed?"

"Hell...I mean, heck yes, Little Bits. Come on. Get that little fanny of yours movin'." Chloe relaxed, more comfortable with the teasing Ed than the kindhearted one.

We went to our place, and Ed went to get Mom. I offered Chloe a soda. When we were out of soda in the kitchen and I went to get a case from the basement, Mom and Ed's voices drifted to me from the back hall.

"Did he hurt her?"

"No more so than usual. Scared her shitless, that I know." Ed was the only one who got away with cussing around Mom. "It's pretty red. Might bruise some. She had to sell her fucking bike to buy a dress. Uhh...sorry, Mom." The f-bomb was still forbidden.

Mom *tsk-tsked*. "Well, I'll put in a call to Child Services, for all the good it will do. I don't know who Tate Rodgers knows down there." I heard her pick up the phone. "Pretty sad when you know the number by heart," she murmured, dialing it.

Later Mom took Chloe into her room for a while to fix her dress. When Chloe came out a half-hour later, we were sitting around on the couch, swapping old stories. We all had our tuxes on, but the shirts open and ties undone as it was a hot day. When she walked out, I involuntarily rose to my feet. Ronnie and Ed turned to see what I was gaping at, and their jaws dropped, too. Mom had done up Chloe's hair and put a hint of makeup on her. She'd had no one to teach her. Her dress was this sheer, floral material over a silky lavender sheath of fabric. I was having difficulty breathing. Ed was the first to recover.

"You look real nice, Little Bits. Real nice."

She dipped her head. "Thanks."

We headed to the church soon after that, but I kept thinking about her throughout the wedding ceremony and Ronnie had to jostle me several times to remind me to do something. At the reception, I spent most of my time mooning over her from across the room. Finally, Ed and Ron cornered me.

"Why don't you ask her to dance?"

"Who?"

"Who?" Ed parroted. And Ronnie laughed. Ed put a hand on each of my shoulders, bending a little to look me in the eye. "Chloe. You know, the girl you've been drooling over all day?"

I squirmed uncomfortably. "She...wouldn't want to dance with me," I mumbled.

"How do you know if you don't ask her?" Ed turned me, and gave me a little shove in the direction of her table.

Chloe, having sensed something was up, was watching the whole little scene. She watched me approach skeptically with the cutest little wisp of a smile on her face.

"Uhh..." I said smoothly when I reached her, "do you want to dance?"

She peered at me, then around my shoulder at Ed and Ron. I turned to catch them smiling and waving to her with shit-eating grins on their fat mugs.

She looked me in the eye coolly. "Is this your idea? Or did your brothers put you up to it?"

"Uhh..." I swiped my sweaty palms along my pants. "Well...they sort of...suggested it. But I was going to ask you anyway."

"Hmm..." she murmured, trying to judge the truth in my statement. She leaned forward, whispering, "Why don't we really give them something to talk about and leave together."

I smiled, at home now. "I like the way you think." She stood, and I offered her my arm. Ed and Ron watched us walk across the dance floor, but we didn't stop, as they expected us to. We continued on to the door, I held it open for Chloe, then turned and winked at them. They burst out laughing, and hooting. "Way to go, little brother."

We wandered around, and finally ended up on the back stoop of the building, all alone. We sat, and Chloe was quiet at first. Then she burst out with, "I miss my dad sometimes."

"I do, too." I picked a leaf from a nearby bush and ran it through my fingers. "He was a good guy." We hadn't talked about it much. I think she was ultra-sensitive about talking about her dad knowing I wasn't overly-fond of ours, since he walked out on our mom. He hadn't even shown for Ed's wedding, saying, "as much as he wanted to, he couldn't get away from the office," although we all knew he was really with his new wife and kids.

"Yes...he was a good guy," she said with a sigh. She was on the top step; I was on the bottom, leaning back on my elbows. The low *thruum, thruum* of the bass drifted out from under the crack of the door.

"Chloe?" I said softly, squinting up at her as the setting sun got into my eyes.

"Hmm..."

"Are you...okay?"

Her face contorted for a moment and she seemed to struggle to control her emotions, finally choking out, "Yes, Nash. I'm fine. Just tired."

Tired of being alone, tired of shouldering all of it herself, tired of living in fear; I could see it all in her face.

I smiled. "Why don't we go inside and dance."

Her shoulders relaxed and the corners of her lips turned up. "I'd love to."

We walked in as a song was finishing, and people were leaving the dance floor because a slow song was starting. I held Chloe's hand, searching the room for my brothers. Ronnie was sitting at a table, joking around with his friends, but when he saw me, he stopped mid-sentence, his mouth hanging open. I stretched Chloe out dramatically to the end of my arm on the near-empty dance floor, then pulled her in and began to sway with the music. Ronnie's face split into a grin. He mumbled something, jumped up, and went over to nudge Ed, who was flirting with his new wife. Ed grinned, too, lifting his champagne glass to us.

Chloe laughed lightly. "I love your family."

"Yeah. I guess they're all right."

A honk from the bass-thumping car behind me alerted me to the light changing. I stepped on the gas. What had happened to us?

CHAPTER FIVE

Chloe

After Nash left, I continued to gaze out the window for some time, my robe hanging limply around me. I closed my eyes, trying to shut out the memories, but they came anyway.

We came back to the tree house often. One time, the owner came out and chased us away, lecturing us on using other people's property without asking. After that first time, though, I think he saw we were doing no harm to his tree house, and he looked too old to have kids to use it, so he let us stay. I could tell he would come up every now and then to check it out, though, as we would find things moved. Things like Nash's cool, clear plastic bank which was made up of different sized cylinders, one for each denomination coin, reminding me of the pipe organ at church. I know we had other trinkets up there as well, but I can't remember what. Maybe binoculars...or a telescope? One thing was for sure, copies of Trixie Belden books always littered the floor, and several of the familiar, yellow-covered Nancy Drews. Nash even tried to get into the Hardy Boys, but it didn't last long.

We made ourselves a club, stealing a little from my Trixie Belden books, and would signal each other by imitating a bob-white's call, *bob-bobwhite, bob-bob-white*. If Nash would respond with a similar call, then I would know it was safe to come up. We thought about asking other kids to join us, like Trixie had her Bob-Whites, Jim and Honey and Marty and her other brothers, but in the end, we decided we liked that it was all ours.

It was in the clubhouse that Nash kissed me for the first time.

We were...sixteen, I guess. Although we didn't hang out constantly like we used to, we were still good friends. That day, Nash surprised me in the garden.

His voice made me jump and I spun around, accidentally spraying him with the hose.

He glanced down at his dripping clothes, and then looked back up with a wicked grin. "You're going to get it." I dropped the hose, laughing and running, but he caught me in his strong arms, made tight by baseball, and dragged me back to the hose. I fought him as he stuck the nozzle down my shirt, and shrieked at the cold water. Then he poured it over my head, getting both of us soaked in the process as I wriggled in his arms.

My stepdad stuck his head out the window, which, years before, he had cleaned and never bothered to put the screen back on. "You kids keep it down!" he hollered. "I'm trying to watch the game."

We turned the hose off and ran away laughing, our feet automatically taking us to the clubhouse. When we got there, we took a few minutes to catch our breath, but then Nash laughed and said, "Man, you really did get me." He wrung out his shirt to prove his point, creating a tiny puddle on the carpeting. I looked down at my own clothing. I had on my denim Daisy Dukes and a light-blue, button down shirt I tied at the bottom, having undone some buttons to create ties out of the corners of it, as was the style then, thanks, again, to little Miss Daisy. When I looked up, Nash was taking off his shirt to stretch it over the wall in the sunlight to dry. My eyes widened as I gazed on his muscular back. This was *not* the boy I grew up with. He turned and he must have seen something in my eyes, because he walked over and rubbed my arms. "You're awfully wet, too. Maybe you should take *your* shirt off?"

"Yeah, right." I laughed it off, but now I could see something in his eyes akin to what he must have seen in mine. I turned and walked to the opposite side of the clubhouse, trying to appear casual and not crazy-out-of-my-head for him, trying to keep my cool. He didn't follow me though. After several seconds in which he did not speak or move, I turned around, curious. He had a strange expression on his face; I couldn't read him.

He picked up an elm leaf, half-orange, half-red, which escaped from its tree and landed on our clubhouse floor. He twirled it thoughtfully. "I heard you went out with Fred Winn..." he said hesitantly.

My face grew hot, but I shrugged, picking up my own stained-glass leaf. "I wouldn't exactly call it a date. I ran into him at McDonald's, and we shared some fries, is all."

He paused, watching my face intently. "That's not what I heard."

"What did you hear?" I asked quickly. Who would have known what happened between us?

Fred had offered me a ride home and shown me "the correct way to eat McDonald's fries," which, according to him, was to dump them out in the bag, add a packet of salt, and shake them up. I had to admit, those were some of the best fries I'd ever eaten, hot, greasy and salty, and delicious. Then Fred suggested a ride through the park, which turned into parking behind the amphitheater. I was too naïve to understand this wasn't the first time he'd come here with a girl, and he had something planned for us the minute he saw me in line at McDonald's. He was a dark, wavy-haired junior with wicked green eyes and a brilliant smile. He was on the swim team, built, cocky, and funny.

He was about to kiss me, when a policeman pulled in behind us and told us we'd have to leave. Fred consented, and the officer followed us out. But Fred turned around and came back in through another entrance. He drove by the amphitheater again, but didn't stop, entering an upper parking lot instead. He turned the engine off, and hopped out, leading me into the woods a yard or two, before grabbing my shoulders and sticking his tongue down my throat. I almost choked. Strangely, he didn't know what to do with his tongue once it was in there. He had me lay and got on top of me, gagging me with his tongue again, and grinding against me in the dirt and leaves. My mind was whirling. What do I do? How should I act? What was he doing? But I quickly made an excuse and had him take me home so I could sort out what happened.

Fortunately, Fred never thought another thing about me, so I didn't need to worry about what to do next. He'd undoubtedly found some other girl to rub against in the park. Someone who understood what it was all about. But I'd told nobody about it, and nobody saw us except for the park ranger. So how did Nash seem to know?

"Who told you about Fred and me?"

"Well, you did for one," he said, sounding irritated. "'Fred and me'? I thought there was no 'Fred and me'?"

"There's not," I said, getting defensive. "He just..."

"He was talking at the lunch table about taking you to the park," Nash remarked, his jaw tight.

I stepped back a few steps, wrapping my arm around my stomach, feeling like someone had punched me. "He...what?" I stammered. How could he?

"Don't worry. No one believed him. He's always talking about his conquests," Nash reassured me, but he kept looking at me as if he could read everything that happened at the park on my face. "But..." he said slowly, "seeing your face now, I believe something did happen in the park."

I wanted to cry. And I felt like screaming. I didn't want to fall apart in front of him, so I settled on the latter. "You know, Nash this is none of your business. I didn't realize you'd turned the clubhouse into an interrogation center. I don't need to answer your questions." I grabbed the top of the ladder and made a move to descend.

"Wait!" he cried. "I'm sorry, Chloe. You're right. I shouldn't be prying into your private life."

I hesitated, then crossed my arms and moved to look out over the trees and the creek. After a moment of silence, in which I tried to steady myself, Nash put his hands on my shoulders. I closed my eyes and leaned into him, absorbing his warmth and closeness, and he slid his hands around to my arms, speaking in a hushed tone in my ear.

"I'm sorry, Chloe. I really am. Don't be mad."

"I'm not mad," I choked out. Then added, "Anymore." He chuckled at that.

"Come over here with me and let's lie and watch the clouds like we used to," he murmured, taking my hand and leading me to the biggest open space on the rug. We laid down, side-by-side, and he took my hand. I turned my head to look at him, and found he was peering at me, his face inches from mine. His gaze roamed over my face and he wet his lips. He reached over and touched my hair. "Do you have any idea how pretty you are, Chloe?" His voice was serious, so I knew he wasn't kidding, but it was all sort of surreal at the time. He sat on one elbow and I watched him. Slowly he bent forward and my heart hammered away in my chest. Gently, he pressed his lips to mine, and then pulled away to see my reaction. I felt...confused. He was my best friend after all. And, I felt overwhelmed by my feelings for him.

He was the only boy who didn't scare me out of my mind. Or make me feel dirty or cheap, or used. He made me feel loved. Fred had made me feel exposed, taken. So had David Williamson, a freshman like Nash and me, who gave me a kiss on the school bus. We were returning from a swim meet. I was the boys' swim team manager. How I was lucky enough to fall into that position, I don't remember. But Fred was on the swim team, and David, and another junior, a diver, named Jeff Baker.

Jeff took me on my first real date, to a nice restaurant where we had burgers, and then back to his house, where we watched a movie and fooled around on his parents' living room floor. He told me, after we'd been seeing each other for a few weeks, as the lights were going down in the movie theatre we went to, what he liked about me was I didn't mind him seeing other girls. I was happy for the instant darkness, as he couldn't see my face and how crushed I was. I had no idea he was seeing someone else. The next day when he called, without even thinking I told him I couldn't go out with him anymore because my "jealous boyfriend from work" was mad about it. I made a boyfriend up because I guess I wanted to hurt him as much as he hurt me. But I was the one crying when I hung up the phone. And that, in a nutshell, was my dating history. Pretty bleak. Guys who wanted to take advantage of me, and who pushed me to do things I wasn't comfortable with.

But here was someone I had loved for a long time, and I was only beginning to see how much now. I reached up and touched Nash's face, watching my fingers as I trailed them down his cheek, and then looking into his eyes, begging him silently to kiss me again. As if in response to my unasked question, he bent once more, covering my lips with his. His lips were soft and skillful. Mine willingly responded to their urging, my heart racing, but not with the usual confusion and uneasiness. A part of me knew I had wanted him since the moment the concept of having a boyfriend first crossed my mind. And now, it felt so warm, so right, like it was always meant to be.

I reached back and threaded my fingers through his thick hair, a leg curling up involuntarily as a tremulous heat ignited in my core, spreading to my toes. His hand grazed my knee, then slid smoothly down my leg, and behind my calf, strong and sure. His mouth began to explore mine more insistently and his hand changed course and glided up the back of my thigh, dipping under the fringed ends of my Daisy Dukes, and suddenly I wanted him to touch me everywhere. I wanted those hands to be the first to discover my body, those lips to be the first to claim every part of me. I wanted to feel his body, too, to learn the things that turned him on, that pleased him. My hand traveled along his bare muscular back, clutching him to me with an urgency I'd never felt before.

His hand slipped lower, coming around the curve of my rear to cup my flesh, his pinky finger drifted and hit the joint of my inner thigh and a small moan escaped from within me. His fingers searched further and all of a sudden I was pushing away from him and telling him no.

"Chloe, I'm sorry," he said, concerned. "I shouldn't have—"

My finger flew to still his lips. "I wanted you to, and that's what scares me," I stated breathlessly, my gaze darting between his eyes to read his reaction. A slow smile spread over his face and his hand moved up to slide underneath my shirt at the small of my back. He embraced me, burying his face in my hair.

"You want me, Chloe Carmichael." He tickled me with his breath and the rumble of his voice, which sounded slightly triumphant. "You want me."

"Yes, Nash, I do," I whispered, inciting him all the more. His hot mouth skimmed along my neck and I squeezed my legs together to stem my growing need and involuntarily arched in his hands. His lips came to my throat and I moaned his name as our mouths and tongues collided again.

I was sure we both heard the man's voice. "What are you kids doing up there?" But instead of stopping, Nash's kisses became more intense, drawing me into him.

"Nash," I tried to cry, but he swallowed my warning, changing angles to awaken a new quaking response in me. "Nash!" The man's boots scraped the tree as he began to climb the ladder. Nash flew up, pulling me with him and moving away. When the owner's head appeared through the hole in the floor, Nash smiled at him innocently. But I was still trying to catch my breath, my face flushed, eyes wide with surprise.

The man looked from Nash, to me, not taken in for a minute. "You two need to get on out of here. This isn't the place for two teenagers to do...whatever it was you were doing," he finished with a wave of his hand, flustered. "Now get on out of here!" he barked.

"Yes, sir." Nash grinned. He stood and moved to the ladder and the older man backed, reluctantly, down. Nash winked at me when the owner was out of sight, but hurried down the ladder. I sat for a minute, stunned, but then scrambled after them. Nash's hand slid unnecessarily up my leg as he helped me down, purposefully brushing my backside as he did so. "Have a good evening, sir." He grabbed my hand and led me off into the woods.

"And I better not catch you back here again," the man threatened. I glanced back over my shoulder apologetically catching the man's gaze for a second or two before Nash swung me around to pin me against a tree, pressing his lips again to mine. I looked sideways to see if the man was still watching us, and he was.

"Nash," I murmured against his lips.

"Get out of here!" the man screamed, red in the face.

Nash laughed and dragged me after him again as we ran through the woods feeling ecstatically, giddily happy.

I closed my eyes remembering the warmth of that kiss and its ability to move me, so unlike when Jack's lips manipulated mine, which were cold and lifeless. Slowly, I opened my eyes. As they came back into focus, I realized the sidewalk below, in front of the empty parking space where Nash had been, was no longer peppered with raindrops, but was, indeed, one smooth, slickly wet surface. Unbeknownst to me, the rain had been coming in my window, making the tops of my feet wet. Looking at the shiny droplets on my feet and on the dirty sill, I pushed the window shut, and drew my robe more closely around me. But it couldn't keep out the chill seeing Nash gave me.

CHAPTER SIX

Nash

As distracted as I was, I didn't notice the cab in front of me slowing down to drop off a passenger. Seeing it too late, I squashed on my brakes, squealing to a skidding stop. My gaze flew to my rearview mirror to see if the driver behind me was paying attention and had time to stop. I watched the middle-aged man come to a jerking stop as he laid on the horn in frustration. Not for the first time, I began to wonder why I left Cold Springs to live in a city of steel and glass and taxicabs and short-tempered drivers.

Leaving Chloe behind in Cold Springs made me feel like a rabbit in a trap that has to gnaw through its paw and leave part of itself behind to break free. I knew I would return to marry her someday, but to leave her, where Tate could continue to fill her mind with crap and do...who knows what else to her, that was a killer. But I couldn't support her on my own yet. I needed the education to earn the money to do so. And that, unfortunately, took me hours away from her to New York City.

I was born in the city, but growing up in Cold Springs from a very early age washed the city stench from me. I found living there depressing and strangely confining, like the enormous skyscrapers were prison guards watching over me, keeping me away from home and Chloe. I got a job at a coffee house, which turned out to be very convenient as it supplied me with the caffeine I needed to stay up and study. Girls would often flirt with me when they came in, leaving their phone numbers on napkins, matchbook covers, or even, once, on the back of a Lynyrd Skynyrd concert ticket stub. But the big-city girls were too intimidating, too forward, and often, too shallow. Not to mention the fact my heart belonged somewhere else. I lived for the weekends when I could steal home and be with Chloe, until my boss kept scheduling me on weekends and I couldn't afford to quit. I kept telling myself every dime brought me closer to bringing Chloe and I together for good, but that didn't make the nights any shorter or lessen the ache I had for her.

It was the same ache gnawing through me now as I sat in an endless line of traffic listening to the cacophony of horn-blowing all around me.

Chloe

I sat all evening and into the night on the couch in my robe, never moving more than to get another bottle. I sat as the room became murky, and didn't even bother to turn on the lights when the world outside became black and all I had for light was the streetlight shining in through the window. I sat and thought about Nash, about the way it felt to be in his arms, about how that was the last time I truly felt cared for. And then I forced myself to think of his harsh words, and the wounds he left me. In the end I curled up on a corner of the couch and fell asleep.

After that first kiss, Nash became my world. He was my lifeline. He was light and breath, in a place where the walls were closing in on me, and I loved him. But he was like everyone else, in the end. He let me down, or I let him down, I'm not sure what the difference was anymore.

My form of escape was to take off with Nash, and spend hours in his arms in the tree house, talking about nothing, counting the stars, simply being together. Tate didn't much like our spending time together, so we had to sneak off. One night...I had made fried chicken for Tate. I took a plate to my mom, even though I knew she wouldn't eat any, and then I did the dishes. The windows were open and I listened for Nash but didn't hear him. Discouraged, thinking he had other plans for the night, I dragged myself outside with the trash. When I opened the lid of the garbage can, taped to the underside was a red envelope. I glanced around with a smile on my face, then dropped the trash and peeled it off. It was one of my first love letters from Nash. He made me feel so special, so worthwhile; I couldn't believe how wonderful he was to me. The last line on the card said simply, "MEET ME." He didn't need to say where.

I threw my trash in the can, clanking the lid down hurriedly and running along the creek. As I did, I thought about the days when we roamed the creek together as kids, in a time which seemed so long ago. When I got to the tree house, he was waiting. I couldn't believe my eyes when I first saw him. He was dressed up in church pants, and a nice shirt. A big bouquet of flowers danced in a vase he must have stolen from his mom, alongside it was a little, battery-operated radio. That's when I remembered it was Prom Night. My stepfather told me "no child of his" was going to any dance and "whore around with a bunch of good-for-nothings." I told Nash he should go with someone else, but he lifted my chin, and kissed me, and told me there was no one he would want to go with when he could spend the night with the most beautiful girl in the world instead.

"Oh, Nash," I cried when I figured out he created our own little Prom Night for us. I smiled through my tears. "You look so handsome."

"And you look...*fantastic*." He drew me to him and kissed me, ignoring the blush which rose to my cheeks.

I pulled away finally. "Oh. You look so nice, and I look...ugh." My gaze roamed over my worn Daisy Dukes, which were out of style by that time, but Tate wouldn't let me purchase any new clothes, and I hadn't even bothered to put on any shoes. My feet were filthy, and I undoubtedly smelled like fried chicken.

"You look great to me." He reeled me in for another kiss, but I squirmed away and walked to the other side of the tree house, agitated.

"You should be out with some real girl and not be wasting your time here with me."

He sidled up and slipped his arms around me from behind, trying to tease away my mood. "So you finally admit you're not real. You are only a figment of my fantasies."

I pushed away from him again. "Nash, stop. I mean it. I'm keeping you from having a normal life with some girl who would be good for you."

"Dammit, Chloe! Don't talk like that," he spat. "Don't you go talking that trash he spews out at you. You know you're better than that."

But sometimes I wondered. It was so much easier to disbelieve the awful things Tate said about Nash, than to doubt the things he said about me.

Nash turned me to face him. "When are you going to get it through your thick, pretty head," he said, tapping my temple, "*you* are the only one for me, Chloe Carmichael?" He kissed me softly and I melted into the kiss. "I love you," he said as he pulled back briefly.

"Mmm," I murmured, my eyes still closed. "If you weren't such a good kisser, maybe I'd be noble enough to give you up for your own good." I opened my eyes, smiling at him.

He grinned broadly, knowing he won the argument for the night; I was much too weak. "Dance with me," he ordered, leading me out onto our green-carpeted dance floor. The music droned quietly as we swayed together, a gentle breeze fanning us. I laid my head on his chest, and listened to his heart beat, knowing that, for tonight, it beat for me.

A week later we were up in the tree house again. It was late spring, and Nash's pebble had pinged off my window earlier in the morning than usual. In fact, I was still sleeping. I rolled out of bed with a smile and tugged my Keds on. I had slept in my clothes, so I only needed to brush my teeth, and amble out the back door. He took my hand wordlessly and we walked, afraid to break the early morning stillness. A single bird chirped in the tree branches along the creek happily, as if greeting us along our path. We talked quietly after a while, but Nash seemed distracted, and unusually quiet.

"Why so silent this morning?" I asked curiously, turning my head to take in his expression.

He laughed. "Am I?" Then he fell into another lapse of conversation.

I continued to study him. "Come on. What's on your mind?"

"Nothing, nothing," he answered evasively, but then he buckled under the weight of my gaze. "I was just thinking about..." He trailed off for a moment, then, picked up the thread of his conversation. "Do you know what Mr. Dykes said to me yesterday?"

"That you were a massively talented artist and you should pursue that?" I answered quickly. Nash's artwork, which was always amazing, had really taken off under Mr. Dykes' tutelage. The young teacher had come to our school two years ago.

He blushed. "Something like that," he mumbled. "And he told me he entered me for a scholarship to the New York School of Art."

"Oh," I breathed, suddenly dizzy, my hands going clammy.

"But, of course, I wouldn't go, even if I won it. I couldn't go that far away from you."

"No. No," I struggled out. "You should consider it. I'll always be here for you," I added. But deep down I feared if he went away, he would find someone new. Someone bright and witty, a talented artist such as himself. Someone pretty, capable of making him happy. Part of me wanted that for him. Part of me dreaded the black hole which would open up if he left me.

"I know you will," he replied lightheartedly, squeezing my hand. "But I would miss you too much."

I should have argued with him, but my throat was tight.

About a month later I found him in the same reticent mood. We were lying on the floor of the tree house this time. It was night, probably about nine. Nash was on his back, had one arm around me, one curled behind his head. I was on my side with my head on his chest, one leg flung across him, my eyes closed, nearly asleep. As I listened to his quiet breathing, I realized he hadn't spoken for some time.

"Nash?" I murmured sleepily. "What are you thinking about?"

"Huh?" he responded, his hand gliding up and down my arm reflexively. "Oh...nothing."

Something in the way he said it had me sitting up on my elbow, blinking my eyes and trying to read his face. Plenty of light illuminated it, thanks to a full moon, and I could see something was troubling him. "What's up?" My heart climbed into my throat.

"Nothing, nothing," he reassured me, pushing back a stray hair which had fallen into my face.

I looked down, straightening his shirt without really thinking about it. "Don't lie to me."

"What? I wouldn't—" He sighed. "Okay, it's...Mr. Dykes told me I won that scholarship today."

My hand stilled on his chest. I knew he was watching my reaction, so I purposefully kept my face neutral. "That's great." I tried to fill my voice with the enthusiasm I didn't feel. He read right through me.

He pulled me back into his arms. "It's okay, Clo. I'm not going."

I could hear the disappointment in his voice. I pushed up again. "No. You should go. It's only...how many years?"

"Four."

"Four," I repeated. I laid my head down, afraid he would see the tears in my eyes. "Four isn't bad." I couldn't help it. I began to cry.

"Clo! Don't do that. I'm not going anywhere, honey. I'm staying right here with you."

But I knew I couldn't do that to him. We argued for hours, me telling him he couldn't waste this opportunity, he saying it didn't matter to him. But we both knew it did. In the end we decided he would go away and come home on the weekends. It was only a three-hour drive. Our love was strong enough to endure. Or so we hoped.

The day he left was probably the hardest I'd ever known. Even when my dad died, Nash was there for me; but now I was utterly alone. We kissed through our tears by the side of his truck, not caring if Tate or his mom was watching. He climbed inside, and his truck door slamming shut was like a death knoll. He promised to write and call. I promised to do the same. But we both knew this could be the end.

He called me four hours later, telling me he was forced to pull over twice on the way there to cry and it was killing him to be away from me. That night I cried myself to sleep on the clubhouse floor, curled up in the fetal position in the cold, trying to find his scent on the carpet, but smelling only wood and dirt.

Chloe

In the weeks following Nash's leaving for school, I went mechanically through my days, waiting for the postman and taking his little treasures back to the clubhouse with me to peruse in private. I read and re-read Nash's letters, smeared though they were by my tears, and found an old, wooden box which had been my father's to keep them in, leaving it in one corner of the clubhouse.

One night, at about this time, Tate informed me I was to have a date with his boss's son. Tate, who always told me I was a good girl and shouldn't hang out with the guys around town, set me up with his boss's son, and made it clear I was to make sure he had a good time, "whatever that entailed." Zach Connery took me out to a nice dinner. He opened the car door for me after we left the restaurant, saying, "My sign is Virgo, and I am one. But I'll do anything other than that." He closed the door and I watched him walk around to the driver's side wondering, "What the hell does that mean?" I was so naïve.

When we got back to the house, Zach suggested sitting on the porch swing for a while and "talking," which quickly turned into feeling me up. I knew Tate was right inside the house. The front door was even open, to let in the breeze. I remembered his warnings. "Zach had better have a good time," or my stepfather's "ass would be grass" which would mean mine would be grass, too. I wasn't exactly responsive to Zach's advances, but I tolerated them. He finally took my hand and forced it down his pants. I knew so little about sex, I didn't even understand what he wanted me to do, until he literally had to move my hand up and down over his penis. Catching on, sort of, he let me go so he could sit back and enjoy himself. I was totally grossed out and wanted things to get over with,

so I started moving my hand quicker and quicker, yanking on him unintention-
ally.

"Uhh..." He grimaced, laying his hand over mine on top of his jeans. "That's
too hard."

"Oh. Sorry," I replied lamely, slowing things down.

After a while he said, with a hint of condescension. "You can stop now."

"Oh. Okay."

"I'll need a towel," he said, like I was the stupidest person on the planet.

I wondered what for, until I removed my hand from his pants, and found it
covered in goo. "Uhh. I'll be right back." I marched in past Tate, who was staring dully at the TV but looked up as I went past.

"Having a good time?"

"Peachy," I growled. I grabbed a dish towel and walked back past Tate, who
looked up again curiously, but didn't say anything. I walked out and handed the
towel to Zach, who immediately began to clean himself up.

"Want to go to a party with me? Tommy Egberts is having a party."

Tommy Egberts' parties were widely known to be drunken orgies. "I'm
tired."

"Oh. Okay, then. Goodnight." He handed me the towel, and turned and
headed down the stairs without further comment, whistling some nameless
tune.

I stared after him in silence, and then went inside and straight to the bathroom. I peeled my clothes off and noticed some of the white gook from Zach's
pants was on my favorite purple sweater. I threw it down the laundry chute in
disgust, knowing I would never wear it again, and stuffing my white pants after
it, along with my bra and panties. I soaked in the tub for over an hour, thinking
about what happened and feeling dirty and cheap.

Tate came by at one point and rapped on the door. "Did you show him a
good time?"

"Leave me alone."

He chuckled coarsely and moved on by. I sat in the lukewarm water and
cried.

The next morning I woke to find Tate standing over me with the purple
sweater in his hand.

"What's this?" he screamed.

Terrified, I sat up on my elbows. "I don't know." I was barely awake.

"Well, I'm pretty sure I do," he said suggestively, and then he did something he had never done before, pushing things further than he ever had. He unzipped his pants and stroked his penis with my sweater.

"Mom!" I screamed in horror. Their bedroom was directly across the hall and she could see into my mine from her bed and see what he was doing. She looked at him dully, then turned over and pulled the covers up. Tate was making sick noises now, and calling out to me.

"Was this what it was like Chloe-girl? Huh? Was this what it was like, or did you use your mouth? Maybe you could show me..."

"NO! NO! GET OUT! GET OUT OF HERE!" My gaze flew around the room frantically and landed on Nash's baseball bat, which he left with me in case of emergency. I figured this qualified. I lunged out of my bed and held it aloft. "*GET OUT!*"

Tate only laughed, he was done anyway; a steam of white marked my carpeting. He threw the sweater on my bed. "All right. Calm down." He chuckled. "I'll leave you alone," but as he passed me, he ran the back of his hand down my face, staring at me intently, his eyes hard. "This time."

When he left, I dropped the bat from my shaking hands and curled up with my back to the door, rocking. That night my mom took a lethal overdose of her meds and left me alone with Tate for good.

CHAPTER SEVEN

Chloe

Nash came home for my mom's funeral. I thought about telling him what happened that night, but Tate appeared to be truly despondent over my mom's death, so I believed he'd never do anything of that nature again. Besides, I couldn't bring myself to tell Nash, or to even think about it. It made my skin crawl.

Nash had to go back to school, but after my mom died, he decided he would call me every night for a while to check in on me, which I thought was sweet. And he did call...up until the point I wasn't there to answer his call.

It was five weeks after my mom's funeral. At a quarter to nine, Tate insisted I mow the lawn.

"But it's pitch-black outside."

"You should have thought about that earlier."

"I didn't think about it because I didn't think the lawn needed it. I still don't. I mowed it the day before yesterday."

"But it rained yesterday," he growled. And before I could counter, he threatened, "Now I'm not gonna take any flak from you. Get out there and mow the lawn before I have to toss you out there. 'Cause, believe me, I'll make that awfully unpleasant for you." He rubbed his hands.

"But Nash is going to call," I ventured, backing away just in case. "Can't I wait and do it after I talk to him?"

"You talked to that little son-of-a-bitch last night. What could you possibly have to say to him?"

"Please," I begged. It was hard enough being away from him. I wasn't sure I could take having to go without hearing his voice. "I'll do it as soon as I get off."

"At ten o'clock at night? The neighbors will be sleeping."

"But it's only Mrs. Nabry. What if I ask her?"

"No, dammit. Get your scrawny little ass out there and mow the god damn yard."

I glanced out the back window. "I won't be able to see anything."

He grabbed me by the shoulders and spun me, pushing me forward to kick me in the backside. "I'll turn on the fucking porch light for you. Now *get going*."

I knew by his tone he wasn't about to change his mind on the subject, so I walked out the back door, letting the screen slam behind me, blinded by tears. When I finished mowing and came back in, Tate taunted, "Your little boyfriend didn't even call, Chloe-girl." I hated it when he called me that. "He's no doubt found himself a college girl who is better in the sack than you are and will keep him happy." He sneered, having echoed my own thoughts. As if to confirm this assumption, nothing was waiting for me in the mailbox when I returned home from school the next day, or the day after either. I was heartbroken.

Two days later, Nash's truck screamed into the driveway as I was getting off the bus. I squealed joyfully and hurried down the steps. But as I ran toward him, I could tell something was wrong. He got out of the truck, slamming the door shut, and glaring at me with his hands on his hips, unquestionably furious.

"What the hell, Chloe? I leave for a couple of months and you've already moved on with your life? The least you could do is tell me yourself."

"Wh-what? What are you talking about? I never—"

He smacked his hand on top of his bedliner, making me jump. "Dammit, Chloe! Don't lie to me." I could see the angry tears in his eyes, but I was confused. What was this all about? He turned around and got back into his truck, mumbling, "I don't even know why I bothered." He swung the door shut with a *bang* and started the engine.

"Wait, Nash, please!" I shouted, dropping my books in the grass and moving up to grip the edge of the window he had rolled down. He glared at me and threw the truck into reverse. "I swear, Nash. I have no idea what you are talking about."

"Did you forget I would be calling? Or did it not even matter to you?" he screamed. He stepped on the gas and yanked the wheel.

I had to jump out of the way to keep from getting run over, but my mind found something to wrap around as it was spinning. "Call? You mean Tuesday night? You didn't even call. Tate told me."

"Yeah, right." The truck swerved and slid to a stop a few feet from me, angled to race down the driveway, his face the picture of rage. "Tate told you I didn't call? *He* was the one who picked up the phone when you were out messing around with some other guy."

"Out messing around..." I stammered. "I was out mowing the stinking grass. He told me you didn't even call. That you'd probably found someone "better than me" and then you proved it by not calling or writing."

"I wrote you every day."

"Well, I didn't get any—" Slowly it dawned on me. I wasn't around each day the mailman arrived, but Tate was. He came home from his job at the mill for lunch each day. "Oh, my—" My eyes flew to the house. "He... Oh, my gosh." I was too stunned to catch Nash's expression, but he must have figured out what I had as he slammed the truck into park, and hopped out, leaving it running and heading toward my house.

"I'll kill the son-of-a-bitch."

"No. No! Nash, don't!" I grabbed his bicep as he blew past me but he only dragged me along through the loose gravel. "He'll kill you."

He tried to detach my hands. "Chloe, if you haven't noticed, I'm not a little kid anymore. I can take him."

A wave of panic made me nauseous. "No, Nash, please. He won't fight fair." I began to bawl. "Please, Nash, please." My heart was ripping in my chest. "Don't do this."

He stopped finally and turned to me, putting one of his big, clumsy hands on my face, already wet with tears. "He was trying to mess with us, Chloe. I believed him." I could tell this is what upset him most. "I'm sorry, Clo." He laid his forehead on mine, his remorse palpable. "I should have never believed a word that lying bastard said." He closed his eyes as tears rolled down his face. "I should have never believed him. I'm so sorry. I really am. Can you ever forgive me?" He cupped my face in his hands and raised it so he could read my answer.

"It's okay, Nash. He made me doubt you, too. He made me think you'd found someone else."

He started kissing my face. "There will never be anyone else. Never."

"Okay," I responded breathlessly. "Okay." I closed my eyes, swallowing his words until they lay deep within me. After a moment my eyes came open, caressing his face tenderly. "Take me somewhere. Somewhere away from here. If only for a few hours."

"I could get a hotel room," he said automatically.

For an instant, a flash of fear zipped through me. Then, I made a decision. "Yes. I need to be with you."

He nodded, his face serious. We walked back to the truck, and he held the door open for me. I climbed in behind the wheel, and then scooted over to make room for him. We drove to the L and L Motel, which everyone in town called the "Love 'em and Leave 'em." They had hourly rates. "I'm sorry," he said, switching the engine off, and looking at me. "I can't afford a nicer place."

"This is fine," I answered quickly. "It doesn't matter." He got out and I moved to open the door on my side.

"Wait," he called, through the still-open window. "I'll get it." He opened the door for me and offered his hand. I took it and slid out to stand in front of him, gazing up at his face with a smile. He swallowed, playing with my hair for a second. "Are you nervous?"

I shook my head. "Not with you." My words became choked. "Never with you." He seemed to relax.

"I'll go pay. You stay right here." He was back within minutes, a big smile on his face. The manager gave him the keys to the room we were parked in front of. I took that as a good sign. He opened the door, and stood back so I could go in.

The room was dark, and kind of depressing, with long, heavy drapes at the windows and mirrors along the back wall, next to the bed, with black "cracks" designed in each pane. I ran my hand along the dresser, watching the gray dust accumulate under my fingers, but the wood underneath was, oddly, a rich cherry. I could feel him watching me. He set the keys on the dresser behind me and I turned to him.

"You okay with this?"

I nodded, though I was a bit nervous now. Not about him, but about my own abilities to please him. But when he drew me in to kiss me, all worries flew out the window. He led me over to the bed, looking at the mottled burgundy and black comforter doubtfully. "Maybe we should lie on top of it."

I nodded, and we sat next to each other, suddenly awkward. He bounced up and down a little, as if testing the springs. "Good bed," he commented with a tenuous smile. We went to kiss each other, and bumped noses, and then got our hands tangled up, going in the same direction as we tried to put our arms around each other. He laughed, with a snort, and pushed me backward, playfully straddling me and that's when I knew it would be okay. No matter how bad I was, Nash would laugh about it and teach me to do better.

"I love you, Nash."

"I love you, too, Chloe." He kissed me, threading his fingers through mine in an innocent way. Then, he slowly, sensuously spread our hands out in a circle to bring them over my head. He locked both of my wrists in one of his big hands, and in that position, lying vulnerable beneath him, totally controlled by his desires, I melted to his will, gave myself up in my need to be everything to him. He brought his free hand down to the small of my back, where he found skin as my shirt was bunched up beneath me. "Scoot up on the bed more," he requested against my lips, and then he rolled off, releasing me and moving all the way onto the bed so his head was against the pillows and he was aligned with the bed correctly. He tugged on his shoes, and when he'd released them, pitched them into the dark corner of the room blindly. I watched him, slipping off my own Keds and leaving them neatly by the side of the bed. "Come here," he growled, with a smile.

I moved up and knelt beside him. Lifting my hands, I slowly unbuttoned my shirt, while at the same time moving to straddle his hips. He watched me, looking like he was not even daring to breathe. When I released the last one and made a move to remove my shirt, he quickly reached up to snatch my hands. Seeing the startled look in my eyes, he brought my hands wordlessly to his lips, and kissed each one, then let them go and brought his hands to grasp my hips. Again, I relished the sensation he was in charge of me, his big hands tightly holding my center. Slowly, ever so slowly, painfully slowly, he brought his hands underneath my shirt and touched my bare stomach. I sucked in my breath, incredibly turned on, and he looked into my eyes with a wicked grin that said, "Hold on. I'm just getting started."

He brought his hands up, travelling over my stomach, between my breasts, which seemed to pulse beneath my skin, and then he laid them flat on my upper chest for a second before looping out, pulling the fabric of my shirt open, and then off. I suddenly wished I had worn my lacy black bra, instead of my plain one. But as he explored, I was happy with my ample breasts which seemed to fill his hands to overflowing. I pressed myself into his palms, having dreamt of him caressing me this way for so long, and I couldn't take it any longer. I flopped over him and began to feverishly kiss his lips. Incited by my passion, he grabbed me and flipped me so he was over me, pressing his hard pelvis against mine. He moaned, shifted, and fumbled with the snap of my jean shorts, finally undoing it and yanking the cloth apart so the zipper was forced down. He slid his hands behind me and cupped my backside, his hands gliding over my silky panties. Making a noise in between a grunt and a moan, he yanked on my shorts, wedging them down from side-to-side until he got them off my heels and threw them across the room.

Sitting, he whipped his shirt off over his head. He stood beside the bed while I watched, sliding his jeans off to the floor in seconds, and managing to get his socks off with them. He was back on top of me before I could blink, both hands squeezing my breasts, his fingers finally clawing the fabric away and teasing my nipples in a way that nearly sent me over the edge. He fell forward, his face in my hair, his breath coming rapidly. "Oh, God. How I want you, Chloe."

He began to kiss my neck and I couldn't believe the sensations which rocketed through me. My hands were intertwined in his hair, and he moved them again so they were over my head, against the headboard, trapped in his hand. Placing his free hand between my legs, he pushed aside the fabric of my panties and his fingers plunged into me. I moaned rhythmically, with each strong thrust of his hand, arching my neck, where his mouth and tongue continued to sample me, his teeth occasionally biting into my shoulder. And then his mouth was again at my ear, his breath shuddering. "I want to be in you, Chloe. I want to be in you."

I pressed my hips against him. "Yes. Yes." He smothered my cries with his mouth and let go of my hands, which came down to squeeze his rising and falling butt as his pelvis grinded against mine. Then he took my hand and laid it flat against his penis and I could feel how long and hard he was and I squeezed him, crying out again in pleasure.

Then something changed. "No," he said weakly, though he still continued to rise and fall. I'm not sure if he caught sight of us in the mirrors, or what made him change his mind, but he breathed jaggedly. "This isn't right." With effort he plopped to one side on the bed.

One of my knees curled up, and I flung a hand over my head, trying to bring my breathing down. Tears of desperation came into my eyes and I fought to control myself.

"I shouldn't have brought you here." He shook his head. "I thought it would be okay to be alone together for a while, but I should have never—" He looked over at me. "Oh, Chloe. Why are you crying? Oh. Don't, babe." He rose on one elbow, his glorious chest muscles rising and falling with each breath as he tried to calm me.

"D-did I do s-something wrong?" I sobbed, my racing hormones suddenly taking a backward turn.

"Oh, no, honey," he cried out, wiping the tears from my face frantically. "No, Clo. You did nothing wrong. *Nothing.* Believe me," he chuckled, "I want you. But not now. Not this way. When we're married. When we're man and wife. *Then* I'll make love to you."

I blinked. "You w-want to m-marry me?"

"Well, of course." He laughed, but then hurriedly added, "I want to wait a year or two, until I have at least half of my college education behind me. But, yes, I want to marry you."

"But," I said hesitantly, "you haven't really dated a lot of girls, maybe you just think I'm the one for you. Maybe there's—"

He put a finger over my lips. "Can I help it if I found the right girl first? Besides, I did date a few girls before we started going out. And, believe me, Chloe Carmichael, they couldn't hold a candle to you." He kissed me tenderly.

"But...what about...we almost..."

"It's... I guess I was too out-of-my-head with the idea of losing you. I... sort of...let myself get carried away. I shouldn't have done that. It was wrong."

I laughed. "If it was so wrong, how come it felt so *right*?"

He put his forehead on mine. "You think so, Miss Chloe?" he teased. "You think so?" He nipped at my lip playfully, nearly getting me started again.

"Yes. I think so, you goof."

"Well." He swung to a sitting position and leaned over to grab his jeans from the floor. "I'm sorry to have got you all going, and everything." He slid his legs into the jeans. "But I'm not going to give into your demands until our wedding night."

"*My* demands." I moved to leave the bed. He dove and caught me around the waist and pulled me back.

"Yes. Your demands." He began to kiss me. "Your sweet...incessant...demands." He punctuated each part of the sentence with a kiss, and then ended with one that took my breath away, his arms wrapped tightly around me, my breasts pressing against his chest. He released me finally, then stretched my bra out and took one final look at my breasts. "Umm...well, I've got to get going. No more time for you to seduce me."

I slapped his chest as he moved away and then groaned. "Oh, do you have to go so soon?" I sat and hugged my knees, looking at him soulfully.

"You know I do," he replied, looking around for his shirt. "I've got a three-hour drive ahead of me."

"But, couldn't you get up early and drive back in the morning?"

"And have Tate Rodgers send the C.I.A., the F.B.I. and the Firearms and Tobacco people out after me?"

"He won't care," I said quickly. "He won't even know. I've spent several nights lately in the clubhouse missing you, and he didn't even notice."

"Really?"

I nodded, hopefully.

He cocked his head. "And you won't try to seduce me?"

I smiled easily. "I make no promises."

He shrugged. "I guess I'll take my chances." He flopped on the bed so hard he almost toppled me off like a trampoline game of "Break the Egg," but he caught me and kept me from falling. We towed the comforter off the other bed and wrapped up in it, his arms wound tightly around me, his mouth by my ear.

"What are we going to do about Tate?" I asked in the gathering darkness. "We won't be able to talk to each other when you go back."

He thought about it. "I'll call my mom's house. You go there at nine o'clock and we'll talk that way."

"Sounds perfect." I sighed, drifting off to sleep in his arms. Around midnight we woke, ravenous, and snuck out to an all-night diner for burgers and fries. As the sun came up, I kissed him goodbye outside his truck a quarter-mile from my driveway.

"I'll call tonight," he promised softly.

"I'll be there."

And I was. That night, and the next, and the one after that. Pretty soon, though, Tate figured out what I was doing. One night I showed up about fifteen minutes late with a swollen eye and a bloodied lip, and a cut opened up over one cheekbone. When I walked in, Mrs. Nabry's eyes grew wide. I held a finger up to my lips and took the receiver.

"Hi, babe."

"Hey, hon. How are you?"

"Good, good." I gave Mrs. Nabry a warning glance, as she still stared at me with her mouth hanging open. "How are you?"

Always true to her word, Mrs. Nabry promised never to tell Nash about that night, and she didn't. Of course I made up some excuse to tell her, supplying a story as to why Tate beat me was easy, as he had done it so many times before. I offered her one of those reasons, afraid if Nash were to find out the truth, Tate laid into me when he discovered I was going over to the Nabry's house to receive Nash's phone calls, he would have undoubtedly come home to face Tate, and I couldn't have that. As it was, that little scenario was always imbedded in my nightmares. I could take Tate beating me; wounds like that healed. But if Tate ever hurt Nash because of me? I couldn't stand that. It would haunt me forever.

So, we kept seeing each other. Nash would come home most weekends, and, although I missed him terribly, I thought maybe we could make this thing work. Yes, I thought then our love could weather any storm.

But now I knew how wrong I could be.

CHAPTER EIGHT

Nash

I drove slowly now through the rain-slicked streets, no longer having a Ferrari to follow. After a thirty-minute drive which should have been a twenty-minute drive, I pulled my truck around the back of my building and parked it in its traditional spot by the dumpster. When I had trudged up the fire escape to my place I closed the door behind me and leaned against it, exhausted. The walls were bleakly white, despite the brightly-colored canvasses stacked one in front of the other along the baseboards. This place had never been home. The only place which could ever be called home was somewhere with Chloe, so I guess that left me a roaming nomad.

With a sigh I swiped a hand across my face, massaging my eyes briefly, trying to forget the stricken look on her face. Why had I treated her like that? No matter what she had done, no one deserved to be treated like that. God, how I still loved her.

I crossed the apartment, which wasn't much of a feat, as it was more or less a glorified broom closet, and opened the freezer, reaching in blindly to grab a frozen dinner. I didn't bother reading the instructions; they were pretty much all the same anyway. I slammed it into the microwave, punched the numbers, and opened the refrigerator for a much-needed beer. I downed it and popped another, forgetting about my meal for a minute and flopping down on the couch. I glanced at the water running down the window pane as the droplets *ping-pinged* off the fire escape and I was transported to another time and place.

I was home for Spring Break, and it was raining to beat the band. I sat listening to the rhythmic sound of it as I drifted off to sleep. A second noise started up, out of synch with the first. I sat up on one elbow and listened harder. A tapping again. I snapped on my bedside light and walked over to my window, where the sound seemed to be coming from. I pulled open the shade and must have jumped back a foot.

"Holy shit!"

Chloe knelt on my roof in the deluge, drenched so badly I didn't recognize her at first. I reached for the window and fumbled with the lock, yanking it

open. I unlocked the screen, and pushed it out, reaching to help her in. "Chloe."
She latched on to me, shaking from head to foot. "What are you doing? Are
you crazy? You could have killed yourself out there." Her teeth were chattering,
and although the rain still ran from her hair and down her face, I could tell it
was mixed with tears. She sobbed and I dropped with her to the floor. "Honey.
Honey. What's wrong? Tell me what happened."

She shook her head. "No. I c-can't," she managed finally.

"Oh, honey. You're freezing."

"No. No," she said, trying to calm down. "I'm okay. I'm just freaked out."

"All right. But let me at least get you out of these wet clothes." She didn't
protest and let me fight off the flannel shorts she had on. They dropped to the
floor with a wet *plop*. I could see her legs were pretty scraped up from the shin-
gles, or from climbing the tree. "I'll get you a T-shirt." I dug through my dresser
drawers and brought out an old concert T-shirt. The white cami she had on was
practically see-through in its current condition, so I don't know why I bothered
to turn away, but I did.

When I spun back, the cami had joined the flannel shorts on the floor and
she stood there, still shivering despite the T-shirt. "Come here. Let's get under
the covers." I got in my bed first, and held the covers up so she could climb in
beside me. I switched off the light and drew her close to me, her back against
my chest, wrapping my arms around her tightly.

We lay in silence for several seconds. "You want to tell me what happened
now?"

She was still, but maybe not having to look at me made it easier for her, because she suddenly burst out, "I woke up, and he was in my bed." She began to
sob again.

My body became tense all over. My jaw set in a rigid line. "What?"

"He came in my bed," she repeated, as if in a state of wonder over it herself.
"He t-touched me."

I sat, practically knocking her out of bed, and switched the light back on.
"He wh-what? Where did he touch you?"

But she had her face covered with her hands and was crying hysterically. It
took every ounce of restraint for me to not shake her and make her tell me what
that bastard had done to her. "It's okay," I said calmly, getting up and tugging on
the pair of jeans by my bed. "I'll take care of it."

"No."

I ignored her.

"NO!" She tore at my jeans frantically.

"No. Not this time, Chloe. This time he gets what he deserves." I tried to move away, and she came sliding out of bed, not relinquishing her hold on the waistline of my pants.

"No, please, Nash. Don't leave me. Please don't leave me." She was on her knees at my feet, crying into my crotch and my gut became hollow. "Please don't leave me. I need you. Please." Her speech became fainter and more incoherent.

I sighed, stroking her wet hair. "Okay, Clo. You win. I'll take care of it in the morning." Her tremulous hands released my pants and she fell on her face, sobbing, her shoulders shaking. "Oh, God, babe. Come here." I lifted her off the ground and poured her into the bed, crawling in after her, our knees touching under the covers. "Shh. Shh. It will be all right." I pushed her hair back and kissed her on the lips.

Her gaze searched my face, and then she started kissing me wildly, all over, on my eyelids, on my cheeks, and, then, finding my lips, she parted them forcefully with her own and began to kiss me with a soul-shattering intensity. I wanted to give in. To follow that kiss to wherever it took me. I gathered my strength and pulled away.

"Whoa, whoa, whoa. What's going on here?" I was confused. Unbalanced by the power of her kiss.

"No." She shook her head, her gaze straying to my lips again. "I need to be with you. I need to know this is good. This is right. Right now, or I don't think I'll ever be able to..."

She leaned forward and I gripped her arms to keep her at a distance. "I'm sorry, Chloe. I don't understand."

She put her hands on either side of my face, her eyes bright. "You don't need to understand, Nash. All you need to know is I love you. And you love me, right?"

"Of course."

"Then...let me love you tonight. I need to." She sat, straddling me, and took my concert T-shirt off over her head in the lamplight. I had never seen her bare body before, and it took my breath away. She was so overwhelmingly beautiful. Her hair, still wet, dark and shiny. Her face, stunning even in its desperation.

"Chloe," I said weakly, my final warning.

"Please," she whispered even as she shifted to remove her panties. She slid down my chest, kissing me, and taking off the pants I'd never even gotten zipped. I groaned as her warm breath aroused me as she kissed me through my underwear. She stripped off that last barrier and then sat again on top of me, her heat pressed against me. I closed my eyes as she reached to slide me into her and my grip tightened on her hips. She began to ride me, slowly, sensuously, her hips gyrating to create a playground of dark sensations which had me crying out. When she finished with me, she collapsed, whispering my name over and over again and telling me she loved me. My throat was dry, but I kissed her hair, telling her I loved her and everything was going to be okay.

The morning light streamed into my room.

"Nash?"

It was my mom at the door.

Chloe was laying by my side, one leg stretched over mine, her hair spread out all over my chest. It took me a few minutes to remember what happened.

"Nash? Are you awake?"

In a panic, I spoke up. "Yes, Mom. I'll be right out."

Chloe pushed off my chest, equally alarmed now she was awake. "Your mom?" she whispered frantically.

"Yes."

She scrambled out of bed, snatching her panties and hopping around on one foot while she tried to put them on. I turned over on my side, my elbow on the bed, head in my hand, watching her with a huge grin. "I've got to get out of here." She finally managed to get one foot in, and leaned her hand on my desk to balance as she lifted her other foot. Even in this situation, I couldn't help but appreciate the smooth curve of her hip, the sensual dip of her lower back, her tight butt... And then when she turned, I caught sight of her bloodied knees, and it all came back.

"You're not going anywhere," I ordered her roughly.

"Nash..."

I flew out of bed and grabbed her arm. "You're not going back to him."

"Be reasonable. I can't let your mom see me."

"We'll explain it to her. She'll understand."

"Oh, right," she answered sarcastically. Then, realizing she was speaking too loudly, she dropped her voice and hissed, "She'll understand how I seduced her son—"

"Well, I think I was a pretty willing party and—"

"Nash. Please. I'll go to the clubhouse. You can meet me there."

I deliberated. "Okay."

She nodded, and threw on her clothes.

"I'll make some excuse to my mom and be right out. You wait for me."

She nodded. "I will. I will."

I grabbed her before she could disappear out the window. "I love you, Chloe."

Her smile was radiant. "I love you, too."

I watched her as she made her way over the roof to the big elm and then she disappeared below the roof line. I didn't know at the time that someone else was watching her, too.

I scrambled into clothes and rushed out of my room and down the steps, taking them two at a time. My mom stopped me in the kitchen.

"Uh-uh-uh. Where are you going off to young man? You slept the morning away and now you're going to tear off without eating any of my chocolate chip pancakes?"

I glanced out the back window into Chloe's back yard, but couldn't see anything but the swing set blowing gently in the breeze. "Okay, Mom." I sat and wolfed down breakfast before racing out the back door.

"I hope Chloe at least ate a decent breakfast," she called after me teasingly, knowing the only person I'd be rushing to see was Chloe.

I ran all the way to the clubhouse, my feet slapping against the wet earth, but when I stuck my head up through the hole, she wasn't there. What could have happened to her? And then I knew. I just knew.

My skin turned to ice. Reversing my steps I hurried back along the creek, splashing through it to the other side and slipping up the far bank. When I reached the edge of her back yard, I saw the pool of blood dripping down her back stairs.

"Oh, geez!" I cried, sickened. "MOM!" I took off at a run. As I drew closer to her house, I could see the streak of smashed grass on the lawn where Tate must have dragged Chloe, and the blood, pooled on the top step where he must have struggled to get the door open and get her over the threshold. It dripped, eerily, from the top step to the next one down, and was smeared on the edge of each of the other steps, too.

I yanked the door open, practically tearing it off its hinges, and immediately began to call out her name, although the path of blood which stretched across the kitchen floor clearly led into the living room. I paused a second as my vision adjusted to the dim lighting inside, wondering about the amount of blood she'd lost, and where she might be bleeding from. It was perfectly quiet in the house, and the crystal clear call of a cardinal sounded nearby. I shouted her name again, and followed the bloody trail to where it ended abruptly two feet into the living room. But it was clear what happened next. The particle-board coffee table was cracked and tilted crazily to one side where I could see one of Chloe's naked, dirty feet, blood speckled all over the top and across the pink-painted toenails.

"Oh, God," I cried brokenly. I stumbled forward and fell to my knees at the end of the table, gazing behind it. She was bent abnormally, upside down, her neck at an odd angle, and I wondered, for a minute, if she was dead. Twisted as she was, I could see her cami was muddy and grass-stained on the back, and fell to her bust line, displaying her bare stomach where some bruising had already begun to occur. Her shorts were partially pulled down on one side, revealing her underwear. Her face was...beyond recognition. I flashed to her beautiful face as she bent over me the previous night in the light from the lamp I used since I was a kid, as she begged me to let her make love to me. My heart rose in my throat and I pushed away the wreckage of the table. Her feet came down with a dead flop on the floor. I stared at her, not knowing if I should move her.

"Nash?" my mom's voice called tentatively from the door. I turned to look for her and saw my baseball bat leaning against the wall by the backdoor, blood dripping down the handle and wiped on the wall behind it.

"Mom!" The panic made my voice sound young, and frightened, and that was how I felt. She rushed in.

When she her eyes fell on Chloe, she cried, "Oh." She came over to fall to her knees by my side. Another, strangled, "oh!" left her mouth as she stared at her battered body. Then she made some disjointed noises of horror and disbelief. She reached and tentatively moved a hair which had fallen across Chloe's face, drawing back her shaky hands, covered in blood from that brief contact.

I turned to Chloe again, noting for the first time the dark red stain on the side of the couch, directly in line with her head, where she slid to the floor. It was her head that was bleeding so badly. "Stay with her while I call an ambulance," I told my mom. I rose and went to the kitchen to the mustard yellow phone, its stretched-out cord almost reaching to the floor. Lifting it from the hook I dialed 911. I stood in the doorway separating the two rooms as I talked to the dispatcher, then hung up the phone dully. "I'm going to find him," I announced, my voice tainted with ice-cold rage.

My mom lifted her head to argue with me, but then her gaze landed on the baseball bat by the back door. *My* baseball bat. He beat her with *my* baseball bat. Mom swallowed, and nodded. "You go get him." Her voice was high and shaky, eyes red with tears, but still able to blaze with emotion. I didn't say anything else. I simply turned to walk through the bloody aftermath of Chloe's beating and out the door.

I drove the truck straight to the tavern Tate always frequented, with the not-so-original name of "The Bar." I didn't see the shiny, new sedan he recently purchased outside, but I stormed in anyway. People looked up, startled by my hasty entry, and gawked at my disheveled appearance, from the bloodstained knees of my jeans, to the wild hair I'd caught in the rearview mirror, the wind having mussed it on the way over. A gray-haired man behind the bar, in an old white dress shirt over a thin undershirt addressed me. "Can I help you, son?" He leaned, his hands stretched wide, on the top of the counter, sleeves rolled up, apparently in the middle of a conversation with the customer seated across from him.

"I'm looking for Tate Rodgers."

The owner and the skinny, equally-grey-haired man on the stool exchanged glances. I closed the distance to the bar. "Listen. If you know where he is, you need to tell me. He just beat the hell out of his stepdaughter."

"Chloe?" the thin man asked. "He hit Chloe?"

"Yeah. He did a number on her with a baseball bat. So if you could tell me where he is, I'd like to do a number on him." My voice was cold, hard steel and my eyes burned with hatred, the tears I cried on the way over drying to leave behind crystallized edges.

"Why would he hit Chloe?" the old man asked, the shock still evident on his face.

"Because that is what the bastard does for grins." I clenched my fists. "Now where is he?"

"We haven't seen him here," a man spoke up from further down the bar. I looked over. He was scruffily looking, with red-blond hair, wearing a red flannel shirt. I recognized him from town, a mechanic named Ralph Denegan. "But if we do," he emphasized, "we'll be sure to let you have a piece of him, after *we're* done." He spoke with an easy drawl, but I was sure he meant every word he said.

I nodded in his direction and turned to head out to the truck. When I got inside the cab, I laid my head on the steering wheel. The anger that was holding me up drained out of me, leaving me hollow and shaky. I picked my head up and started the engine, pointing the truck in the direction of the hospital.

When I got there, my mother was pacing in front of a long window.

"They took her into surgery," she rattled off when I approached. "They said something about maybe having to remove her spleen to stop internal bleeding. There's swelling on her brain. They're not sure if there's any permanent damage..." She ran out of information to give me, and fell back on the question that had no doubt been plaguing her since she first saw Chloe on the floor. "Why did he do this?" She fell apart then, and I took her into my arms.

Chloe was in surgery for five hours. She was in a coma for three days. Every single minute of those three days I spent telling myself if she ever woke up, I wouldn't wait any longer to marry her, or waste any more time apart. And I *definitely* would never leave her alone with Tate Rodgers again. The guys from "The Bar" trickled in one by one that first day to check on her. Every one of them, and a pack of others, was on the lookout for Tate Rodgers, but it appeared the man was long gone. When Chloe woke, she couldn't think of any place he would have gone to, or any out-of-state relatives who would take him in. But then again, she couldn't think of much without getting crippling headaches.

Chloe insisted I return to school while she recovered in the hospital, and even after she was sent home. She reasoned Tate had not been seen in weeks, and my mom promised to take care of her until she was on her feet again. Once I got back to school, I was deluged with work I missed while I spent time back home with Chloe. Soon, my plans for marriage got buried between a fifty-page paper on Art History and a project to create an abstract sculpture. That was a huge mistake.

CHAPTER NINE

Chloe

"Heya, babe." The tall, dark-haired real estate tycoon leaned over me playfully on the elevator, messing with my hair. He smelled good, no doubt wearing some sort of expensive cologne.

"Heya, yourself, handsome." I smiled winningly at him, trying my damnedest to remember his name. Funny how one tumble in the bedroom of a house we were supposed to be showing to potential clients seemed to entitle a guy to grope you whenever he wanted. Not that I minded. Sometimes I thought if they didn't see me for my body and my ability to get them off, they wouldn't see me at all. And I couldn't stand being invisible. I had to matter to someone, if only for fifteen minutes in the coat room at some posh hotel. As the doors opened, my admirer moved away, clearing his throat and flashing a white smile as another Armani-wearing realtor, Taylor McNulty, hopped on the elevator, giving me a conspirator's wink.

He nodded to my friend. "Hey, Jason."

Jason. Thank you.

"You're lookin' a bit under-the-weather there, Clo," Taylor added, giving me a gentle elbow.

"Yeah," I confessed, hanging my head with what I hoped was a sly smile. "Had myself a little party last night with my good friends Jim Beam and Jack Daniels." *Pretty pathetic.* And the pounding in my head was some consolation prize.

"What you need is a hair of the dog. What do you say to you and me meeting for lunch? Say at The Belvedere?"

The Belvedere was a swanky hotel where Taylor would no doubt be reserving a room for us for a little afternoon delight.

"Sounds...delightful," I said coyly, while Jason looked on with a frown.

"Good then. Call me later and we'll firm up a time," Taylor said as he exited on the tenth floor.

When the doors closed behind him, I turned abruptly to Jason. "You're not jealous, are you, Jason?"

He sulked, looking down at his freshly polished shoes. "Well, yeah. Sort of."

"There's no need to be, you know," I returned, walking my fingers up his chest. He raised his head and I brought my lips to his, and then reached to grab him, hard, in the crotch. I knew they had security cameras on the elevator, but what did I care. Turned on, Jason swung me around and smashed me up against the wall, kneading my boobs and then dropping his head to kiss me there.

I laughed loudly, tipping my head back and running my hands through his hair, while at the same time bringing my thigh up between his legs to rub against him. The bell rang for our floor, and he broke away, panting. I straightened my suit coat and blouse.

"When?" he asked desperately.

"Stop by my office later."

He smiled. "Oh, God, yes."

We walked off the elevator and went in different directions without a backward glance. I smiled to myself. This was turning out to be an okay day, despite its rocky start. Or so I thought. Until I checked my calendar and Nash Nabry's name filled up my morning slots. Was this some kind of sick joke? I picked up the phone and dialed Jack.

"Jack, this is Chloe. Did you—?"

"Fill up your calendar this morning?" he snapped. "Yes. Who is this guy anyway? He requested you specifically."

I massaged my temples, which were throbbing again. "We used to...date. A long time ago."

"Ahh. Well, I hate to say it, but you know that old adage, you made your bed, now you'll have to sleep in it?" I didn't comment. "It applies."

Thanks for pointing that out, Jack. You truly are an ass. I wanted to be angry with him, but I knew he was right. "Yeah," I breathed, rubbing my head faster and harder.

"I would take it, but I get the feeling this guy won't let things drop with you. I tried to tell him you were all tied up this morning, but he said he would wait until you're available. I think you have to bite the bullet and face him."

I sighed. "I know. You're right."

"What's the deal, anyway? You still got the hots for this guy or something?"

I had to smile a little at the irritation I sensed in his voice. "It's just...things ended badly for us."

Seconds ticked away without a response. "I'll rearrange my schedule."

"No, Jack. This is my problem. I'll simply have to handle it. But thanks, I owe you."

"Mmm," he growled. "Sounds promising."

After I hung up, I stared at the phone, his words ringing in my ears. *You still have the hots for this guy, or what?* Did I? I shook my head. It really didn't matter. I wasn't about to let Nash Nabry hurt me again. I'd show up and act like an adult, and if he got out of hand, I'd walk out on him. So I had a plan.

I'm sure it was only the hangover that was to blame for my throwing up into my trash can a few minutes later.

Nash

I watched her from the shadows. She walked into the warehouse tentatively, but then, not seeing me, seemed to relax. Today she wore a black silk blouse with white polka dots and a ruffly collar which vee'd down her front, along with a short, black suit skirt like the one she had on the day before. The building we were in appeared to be an old, abandoned warehouse, on the smaller side, but more than big enough for a studio.

She strode around with her arms behind her back, looking up at the enormous skylights above her head. The light danced in her hair and even the sound her heels made on the concrete floor attracted me to her. I enjoyed my anonymity and the ability I had to watch her. A small smile played around her lips, and I could tell by the light in her eyes she liked the place. In my head, a voice rang out, *Sold.*

"Hi."

She jumped about a foot. "Nash!" she screamed, her hand over her heart.

"I'm sorry," I said quickly, moving toward her. "And not only for scaring you, but for the way I acted yesterday."

She looked like I struck her. Like my being nice was worse than the horrible things which I said in her apartment.

"Look, Nash. We don't have to pretend to get along with each other. I'm simply here to show you some properties, and then we can each go our separate ways again. Okay?"

"If that's what you want," I responded coolly, hurt by her indifference.

For a moment I thought she would respond. She looked at me and bit her bottom lip as if to hold something in. I fantasized about her telling me, *That's not what I want. I want you,* and running into my arms. Instead, she turned into the ice-princess I was certain she wasn't.

"So, I think this place would work out great for a studio."

"I like the skylights especially," I commented, looking at her out of the corner of my eye.

"Yes," she said, almost as a sigh. "I agree. They're fantastic." When she realized she accidentally let some emotion show through, she snapped down the professional visor again, clearing her throat. "And the upstairs is roomy enough. If you wanted to, you could add on an apartment for yourself. It would need a little work..." She trailed off, looking wistfully overhead.

"Can I see it?"

"Of course." She took me forward to a set of wooden steps I hadn't noticed before. I followed her up the stairs, noticing how the fabric of her skirt swished against the golden skin of her legs tantalizingly as she climbed. "These were offices at one point, but I think if you took down a few walls..." I could tell she was excited about the possibilities. "For instance, this one." She placed her hands on either side of a wall which created an office on one side, and what appeared to be a small kitchenette on the other, straddling the rooms so she had a foot in one, a foot in the other. "If you took it down, you could have a nice-sized bedroom in here. Come see for yourself."

I moved over to stand behind her, perilously close. I wasn't even looking at the rooms by this point, only at her. I could smell the sweet fragrance of her perfume, something fairly innocent, with a zap of sexiness mixed in. "This would be my bedroom, then," I murmured. She swallowed. "After I took out this wall." I brought my hands down beside hers, effectively trapping her, and, instinctively, I leaned forward to smell her hair and feel it on my skin. She spun in my hands.

"Don't do that."

I reached to stroke her face, my gaze roaming to her lips. "Don't do what, Chloe?" But when my eyes came back up to gaze into hers, I could see fear in them. Not just fear, terror. She was shaking all over. Feeling sorry for her, I backed off, releasing an arm so she could go. In her hurry to get away from me, her stilettos got hung up on each other and she lost her balance. She grabbed for the counter-top to right herself, but fell anyway. I rushed to her side to help her up.

"I'm okay. I'm okay," she insisted, but I could see droplets of blood on the floor. "I'm just too damned clumsy."

"You cut yourself."

"Yes." She inhaled. "That's one thing you'll have to fix if you buy this place. This counter has a sharp edge."

Quite a bit of blood streaked across her palm. "Let me take a look."

"No, it's fine. It's—" I grabbed her hand without waiting for her permission and turned it so I could survey the damage. The underside of the countertop gave her a cut all the way across the base of her palm. "Here." I grabbed a red bandana from the back pocket of my blue jeans and hurried to tie it around her hand to stem the bleeding.

"How's that?"

She slid her hand from mine and rubbed it. Sweat beaded on her forehead. "Fine. Thank you." She stared at me for a second, then turned and raced down the stairs without explanation.

"Chloe, we should talk."

"Phone my office with your offer," she called over her shoulder. "I have to go."

"Chloe." I ran after her. When I reached the top of the steps I spotted her below. She stopped outside the floor-to-ceiling sliding door, and looked back, and then she was gone.

I tried to catch up to her, but tears marked her cheeks as she got behind the wheel of her car, so I let her go.

I stood in the dusty parking lot, wondering what had just happened, and longing for her like never before.

Chloe

I tore out of the parking lot as fast as possible. I knew it wasn't a very mature reaction, but I gave it my best shot, and I simply couldn't do it. I couldn't stand next to him and not want him so badly my arms ached to hold him. I couldn't look into his face and not see the boy who was my best friend, my only friend, and also the man I came to love. I couldn't listen to his voice and not remember the times it soothed me, and at the same time, remember the recent times when it cut like a knife. And when he stepped up behind me and I got a whiff of that good, solid, clean smell, not the smell of expensive cologne, but the fragrance of soap, and laundry detergent, and man... If I had stayed one minute longer, I would have lost control.

I couldn't be out of control with him, or any other man, for that matter. When you lose control, you allow yourself to get hurt, and I couldn't bear that again. So I ran like a scared rabbit, and felt no shame for it.

When I got back to my desk, the phone was ringing. I dove for it.

"Oh, good. I'd almost given up on you."

"Taylor. How's it going?" I responded, slipping naturally into my seductive tone.

"A lot better now that I hear your voice."

"Mmm...me, too," I murmured, coming around my desk to plop into my chair, which rolled back several inches.

"So, I got us a table...and a room, at The Belvedere."

"What time do you want me there?"

"How about right now?"

I smiled. "I think I can swing that."

Taylor already had a bottle of bubbly open on the table when I got there.

I smiled as I scooted around the booth to sit by him. "What are we celebrating?"

"I sold a five-million-dollar house."

"No kidding?" I lifted a glass to clink it against his and downed half of it. "Congratulations."

"Whoa. Whoa, cowgirl. You keep drinking like that and you'll be under the table before the meal even arrives. And I've got some plans for you."

"Oh?" I responded giddily, the bubbles already working their magic.

He leaned forward and whispered in my ear, sliding his hand down my thigh. "Very kinky plans."

That's what I liked about Taylor; no pretense, straight to the point. "Ahh. The best kind." I giggled, tapping his flute again and finishing my glass off. "Don't you worry about me. Have I ever let you down before?"

"No. Never."

Unlike Nash, a little voice badgered. I drowned out the voice with another glass of champagne.

Taylor rushed through his dinner like a fullback gunning for the goal, but by the end of the meal, my head was pounding full-force again. "Taylor, I hate to do this, but—believe me, I hate to do this—but my head is pounding and I don't think I can..."

He grabbed my hand. "Oh, poor baby. Well, we'll just go up and lay down for a while."

"Uh-uh. Last time I 'laid down' with you it was a marathon event, if you remember."

He laughed, lifting my hand to kiss it. "I remember, all right."

"So—"

"Let me give you some—" He fished in his jacket pocket, bringing out a prescription bottle. "—ibuprofen and, I promise, if you still feel bad in a little while, I'll take you home. But my bet is you'll be feeling fine."

He handed me two large yellow pills. "You're sure these are ibuprofen?" I eyed the bottle with suspicion.

"Sure," he responded confidently. "I keep a few in here for my migraines instead of hauling a big bottle around. The bottle's really for my wife's allergy medicine, but instead of throwing it out, I used it."

I downed the pills with ice water, and Taylor grabbed our second bottle of champagne and the ice bucket it was in. "Bill it to Room 304," he called to our waiter as he hurried us out the door.

Once in the elevator, he set the bucket on the floor and put his arms around me from behind. "Chloe, I've waited so long for this," he breathed in my ear, his voice sounding a little strange, like it was distorted, taking on a sort of hollow, ringing quality. "You don't know how often I've thought about you, *fantasized* about you, since the last time." He rubbed his hands up and down my sides. "How's your headache?"

"I don't know," I responded, feeling kind of fuzzy. Did I really drink that much champagne? The door opened on our floor, and I kind of stumbled out.

Taylor laughed. "Looks like somebody's had too much to drink." He put his free arm around me to support me, while he toted the champagne in the other hand, and helped me into a large suite. But by now, I could tell something wasn't right.

"Wh-what did y-you give me?" I couldn't work my mouth right; my lips seemed heavy—not fat, like when you have Novocain, but heavy and slow.

He frowned, yanking his jacket off. "What are you talking about?"

I stumbled forward, and he caught me again. "Wh-what did you give me?" I fought through my panic, forcing the words to come out of my mouth coherently, or at least semi-coherently.

"Calm down, Clo," he snapped. "I gave you something to loosen you up a little. It will make you feel it even better," he added, trying to take my coat off.

"Oh, my God." I jerked my arms out of his grasp, pulling my jacket back up, and almost fell over again, but I was able to scramble away from him.

"Calm down. Everything will be fine. You'll love it, I swear."

By now, the room was spinning, or weaving, or something. "I'm out of here!" I shouted, moving toward what I hoped was the door.

"You're not going anywhere."

He was coming up behind me, so I ran. He grabbed my blouse by the shoulder, and ripped it spinning me around. He pushed me up against the door and kissed my chest, jerking a few of the buttons open. "Come on, Clo. Don't try to fight it."

I was swamped with nausea after being swung so quickly and my eyes kept trying to close. I fought against him. I fought against the dark which threatened to envelope me, and finally, I lashed out. I think I must have connected because he swore and staggered backward. My head cleared momentarily and I got out the door, falling forward, but managing to summon the elevator.

"I think you broke my fucking nose!" Taylor was incensed and coming after me again.

"Oh, please. Please," I begged the elevator. It opened up and I tumbled in, literally at the feet of two teenaged couples inside. They bent to help me up. We turned. Taylor growled at me, blood dripping from his ugly mug, but he whirled around and headed back into the room, slamming the door behind him.

"Are you okay, miss?" one of the boys, who was tall and had dark, curly hair and an innocent face, asked.

"Yes. Yes. I have to get out of here." I could see them exchanging glances over my head. When the elevator opened at the lobby, I made my way out, the dizziness having come back in spades. I felt along the edge of a table, almost knocking over a vase full of fresh flowers, then, made it to a column. The kids had moved on ahead, but the one who talked to me with the curly hair stopped and looked back, breaking away finally and coming to me.

"Do you want me to call someone for you?" He put his arm around me to help me walk.

I needed to speak to him clearly, so I fought through the fog muddling my mind. "I n-need...could you get me a...cab?"

"Sure."

Escorting me through the revolving door was more than a little challenging, but the boy stuck with me valiantly and helped me into the back seat of a cab which was waiting outside. He bent, looking at me sympathetically. "Do you know where you need to go?"

At this point, my mouth was paralyzed, but something in my head was still working. I moaned, but managed to pull out my wallet, which I promptly dropped on the curb. The young man stooped and picked it up for me. It had flipped open, so I jabbed my finger at my license.

"You want to go here?"

I could only groan, not trusting my head to stay on if I nodded it. He turned to the cabbie, sizing him up. "She needs to go to..." he read from my license, "210B Columbine Drive." He looked up at the cabbie. "You'll take care of her?"

"Yeah, sure, Mac. She got money?"

The kids checked again. "Yeah, plenty. And listen," he ducked his head inside to check the driver's tags. "*Raheem*," he said slowly, to emphasize he knew the cabbie's name, "she better have the change when you're done, too."

"She will. She will. What'da ya take me for?" The short, dark-haired cabbie went around to the other side, and the kid crouched, pressing my wallet into my hand.

"Good luck," he said softly, his eyes worried.

"Jimmy," his girlfriend called from behind him, irritated.

The kid stepped back, still watching me, and slowly shut the door.

That's all I remembered.

CHAPTER TEN

Nash

I tried to go home, but all I kept thinking about was Chloe. So, I tried her office on the pretense of offering a bid on the warehouse, but they told me she was gone for the day. I decided maybe our little "close encounter" left her shaken up, so she had to take the rest of the day off. I drove over to her place, and tailgated someone in the door—people were so careless—and knocked, this time more politely, on her door. She wasn't there, so I waited. And waited. And waited. Then, I ordered a pizza to be delivered to my car, and waited some more. I thought about her being off with some other guy, and then told myself she probably went shopping or something. The pizza was delivered, and, although the delivery guy gave me several weird looks, centered on my ordering pizza to my car and not a house, it was some of the best pizza I had since coming to New York.

Hours passed in which I rehearsed a speech for Chloe then rewrote it in my head. I thought about old times with her, good times, and bad. I wondered about where she was, what she must have been thinking... I got out to stretch my legs. I sat on her front steps, and was glad I had worn a T-shirt under my jacket as the sun was getting warmer. I set my jacket on the steps and stuck my legs out on the sidewalk in front of me. A cab pulled up, and I idly watched as the driver came around and opened the door and lifted a woman out of the back, preparing to sling her over his shoulder.

"Oh, man, Chloe!" I rushed up to help him with her as she appeared to be unconscious, but he stepped back.

"You know her?" the cabbie queried.

"Yes. What happened to her?"

"I dunno, Mac. I just drive where they tell me to go."

"She was conscious when she got into your cab?"

"Well..." He shrugged. "Sort of."

I was about to ask him what "sort of" conscious was when he added, "The guy told me where to go."

"She was with a guy? And he put her into a cab like this?"

He shrugged again. "Like I said, Mac—"

"I know, I know, you only drive where they tell you to go." I took the open wallet from her lap and checked it, but it was empty, so I dug into my pocket, and paid the fare. "I'll take her."

"You got it," the Indian man said with a grin, counting the bills I gave him.

I slid one arm underneath her knees and one behind her back and lifted her. "Could you get the door at least?" I asked the cabbie. He frowned, pocketed the money and walked up the stairs, jerking on the door. Right then, the older lady I tailgated in earlier showed up.

"Ma'am? Ma'am?" I said hurriedly.

"Yes?" She turned her twinkly, blue eyes on me.

"This is Chloe Carmichael. She lives in 210B. She's ill. I was wondering if—"

"Of course. Of course." She quickly reached into a dainty little handbag and produced a key card, swiping it and holding the door open. The cabbie took this as his exit sign and tripped off down the steps.

"Gee, thanks," I called to him sarcastically.

"Can I help you? Do you want me to call an ambulance?" the sweet lady asked.

"No, thanks. I think she's just had a bit too much to drink," I whispered conspiratorially. The older woman giggled and put a gloved hand over her mouth.

"My! You're strong," she said as I struggled up the stairs with my precious load.

I looked down the stairwell to where she stood looking up. "I will be by the time I'm done here. Thank you for your help."

"Anytime, hon." She gave me a flirtatious wink.

I grinned as I continued up the stairs. At least I had a fall back plan if I couldn't make things work with Chloe.

But now I was alone with her, I worried maybe I should have taken her to a hospital. I gazed into her face for the first time. Her cheeks were pink, which was reassuring, and her chest was rising and falling rhythmically. It was as if she was in a deep sleep. I looked from her to the door, wondering how I would get it open. I set her on the floor gingerly, and she groaned, which brought a modicum of relief. I fished around in her purse for the key, and then stepped with one foot over her prone body to unlock the door. I stepped back, throwing her purse inside with the keys, and again lifted her, this time grunting as I brought her all the way up from the floor. I bounced her a little, trying to adjust my hold and, as I did, the same Latino man I saw on my first visit came up the stairs with a bag of groceries. His eyes grew wide when he spotted me with Chloe hanging limply in my arms.

I shrugged, as best I could with a hundred plus pounds in my hands. "Too much to drink."

The guy stared at me, completely unconvinced, I could tell. I entered Chloe's apartment and shut the door behind me, hoping he wasn't on his way to call the cops. I laid her on the couch with a sigh, and squatted beside her. I pushed the hair out of her face. "Oh, Clo. What have you done now, babe?" Her skin was warm to the touch, and I sat on the floor beside the couch and watched her breathe.

In some ways, it was surreal to be with her; after all of the time I'd spent thinking about her and wishing, somehow, I could find her. Could she really be here with me now? In some ways, this was the most real experience I'd had in a long time. Life without her was what was strange and uncomfortable. As stilted as our conversations had been, and even painful at times, being with her was being home.

I sighed, drawing my legs up and wrapping my arms around them so I could put my forehead on my knees. Why did I keep goofing up with her? All I wanted was for things to go back to the way they were, before I went off to college. All the time I had been without her, I dreamt of a thousand different conversations where we would sort everything out and get back together. But in real life, the words didn't come easily. Emotions made things messy. And my desire for her made me push too hard, speak too rashly. I lifted my head and reached over to stroke her face again.

We'll get through this. I could tell when she looked at me there was still love there. All we had to do was figure out what went wrong between us. Once we understood that, we could make it all better and get back to where we were. Right? Surely our love for each other was strong enough to see us through this.

Chloe

My eyes opened and a wonderful band of light danced on the ceiling, but my head screamed like a gorilla had been playing tetherball with it. Through the fire of pain, a noise seeped in which was uniquely calming and at the same time infuriatingly annoying, like the whine of a buzz saw. Without even moving it, I knew any movement would jar my head even worse, increasing the riotous hold whatever drug Taylor gave me had over it. Moving only my eyes, I looked down the length of my body in the direction the noise was coming from, and could make out a dark head of hair laying on a pair of arms folded on top of my right hip. I recognized it as Nash's.

Nash. My Nash.

But...not mine anymore. Instinctively my hand reached out to touch his hair, but froze for a second, wavering over the soft, brown, mass. His face was turned away from me toward the window. As if in spite, my hand lowered and I ran my fingers through those thick locks, the silky fibers separating and slipping through my fingers, my nails skimming over his scalp lovingly. I wanted to cry. But then the rhythmic hum of his breathing stopped and I drew back my hand as if burnt. He lifted his head and turned to look at me.

I scrambled up, grabbing my head in agony. "Nash." My wail increased my own pain by the sheer volume of my voice. "What are you doing here?"

"Taking care of you," he snapped. He couldn't have known how my words were highly-influenced by the amount of ringing in my head.

"Well, I don't need anyone to take care of me," I responded foolishly, wincing at the tiny explosions my outburst set off behind my eyes.

"Yes, obviously. Someone put you, unconscious, in the back of a cab, Chloe."

"Oh, yeah...right," I said lamely. I noticed, then, my skirt was unzipped, my shirt untucked. "Who...who undid my skirt?" My voice trembled. I thought I'd gotten away from Taylor...or had the cabbie touched me? A wild panic began to rise in me.

"I did," he mumbled, his face coloring. "I thought you would be more comfortable if I... well...loosened your clothes a little."

I nodded, relieved, and stood, and that's the moment my stomach decided to revolt. My tongue began to sweat and my insides had become a roller coaster. "Oh, man." I lied down quickly. "I think I'm gonna get sick."

"Hold on. Hold on. I'll get a bowl." Nash hopped up and clanged around in my kitchen, the sounds piercing through me like Ninja stars. I closed my eyes, willing the rising bile to stay where it belonged, even as my throat blazed and a new sweat broke out on my forehead. He returned with a big, silver mixing bowl, which would have been exactly what I would have been looking for. "Here," he murmured, putting a hand on my shoulder. He squatted next to me, the concern so evident on his face, I had to turn away.

And then, inexplicably, I began to cry. "Don't do that. Don't look at me that way."

"What way, babe?" He reached to stroke my hair. "I'm not judging you. Although it does worry me some guy might have taken advantage of you in the state you were in."

"See. You are judging me!" I screamed, forgetting for a moment the enemy which waged war within my skull. "You think I let some guy get me drunk?"

His anger returned, not that I could blame him. I was sort of being unreasonable. "Well, yeah, Clo. What else am I supposed to think? You show up here—"

"He drugged me."

His mouth hung open for a moment. A number of emotions crossed his face. "What did you say?"

I wiped my sweaty palm on my skirt. "He drugged me," I repeated quietly.

Again he paused, as if he was letting this new information sink in. "Are you sure?"

"Yes. I had a headache, and he gave me—he told me they were ibuprofen, but—I didn't feel right after I took them. Way too fuzzy. And when I asked him," a small sob escaped. I still couldn't believe Taylor would have done something like that to me. "He told me I would 'enjoy it better' if I was 'loosened up.'"

He jumped to his feet and walked to the window, his back to me, his hands on his hips. "You took what he offered you without questioning it?"

"I th-thought... He told me they were ibuprofen. He's my friend." But I realized now he was no friend at all. He was another guy looking for a good screw, and I was a woman looking to give him one. Wasn't I equally to blame?

"What's his name?" Nash asked, oddly calm. He picked up his jacket from a nearby chair.

My heart rate sped up. "Nash, there's nothing you can do."

"The hell I can't. What's his name?" His voice was so hard it scared me.

"No. You can't—"

"Why not?" he shot back.

"Because..."

"Because why?"

His badgering wasn't making me feel any better. "Just because."

"Because you love him?"

"No."

"Because you want to be with him again?"

"No."

"Because he's such a good friend he gave you a drug which knocked you out?"

"No. Because...I...I..."

"You what, Chloe?"

"Because I wanted to be with him, too," I confessed finally. "I may have led him on."

His jaw twitched. "And that gives him the right to drug you?"

"No. I'm not saying that."

He threw up a hand. "Then what are you saying? He had no idea what that drug would do to you. He could have killed you, all because he wanted to get laid."

"I know. I know," I sobbed.

"Was it Jack?"

"No. It wasn't Jack."

He raised his eyebrows. "Then, who?"

"Just some guy...from work."

"Geez, Chloe. Do you sleep with everyone from your office?"

My jaw tightened. "For your information, I haven't slept with anyone other than you."

He laughed. "Oh, come on."

I flew off the couch, stomping my foot. "I'm telling you, I haven't had intercourse with anyone but—oh. Oh!" The uprising I'd been fighting off surged and I ran to the bathroom and tried to shut the door behind me, but in my hurry, it only banged open again. I reached the toilet barely in time to throw up. I thought about what I'd said. I hadn't had intercourse, it was true, but like Zach Connery, I'd done everything but.

"Chloe...I'm sorry." He came in the door.

"Get out. You can't see me like this." I retched again. "Get out." Tears were running down my face now freely. It was such a strange sensation, to get sick and cry at the same time. I was beyond humiliated now.

"I want to help you."

"Just go. Leave me alone." I folded my arms over the toilet and laid my head on them and lost it. My body shook as I wept, my shoulders aching. Quite a bit of time passed, and I thought he had finally gone, but as I began to get myself more under control, he ran the faucet.

"Here." He pulled my hair back from my face and handed me a glass of water. I sat on my heels and drank the water, grateful for it as it cooled my torn throat and washed away the bitter taste. He flushed the toilet. I didn't want to make eye contact with him. I must have looked a mess.

"Why are you still here?" My voice was a whisper.

"Because...I still love you," he said softly.

I jerked my head up and his easy, open face looked on my kindly. *Why?* He squatted beside me so we were almost eye-to-eye. He looked down for a minute, seeming to gather his thoughts, then, stared me unflinchingly in the eyes. "What happened to us, Clo?" His voice was strained and pain was etched into every feature of his face.

I was blown away. I fell against the tub, my mind filled with a thousand images of him and me, and of things which happened after he left. I shook my head slowly, strangely stunned by him. "I can't do this."

"Can't what?"

"Can't talk about this."

"But we have to talk about it."

With a blinding suddenness, my brain convulsed agonizingly, like someone stuck a steel spike in one ear and out the other. My hands went up instinctively, trying to hold my head onto my shoulders.

"What's wrong? Are you going to be sick again?"

"No," I moaned, my breath coming in quick pants.

"Hey. You're hyperventilating. Calm down."

I nodded as much as my head permitted.

"Maybe I should take you to a doctor."

"No," I squeaked. "I can't handle this right n-now. I can't talk about..."

"Us?" he finished.

I nodded. I glanced up at him.

"Okay." He peeled off his jacket. "But I think you need to get some more sleep."

"You're staying?"

"Yes," he answered simply.

The sweep of relief I felt surprised me. For the first time in a long time I didn't feel alone. At the same time, I was scared to death. What was I doing? I couldn't let him back into my life. But, I also couldn't not let him into my life. The thought terrified me.

CHAPTER ELEVEN

Nash

I set the *New York Times* crossword puzzle on Chloe's coffee table and got up for the fourth or fifth time to go check on her. I stood in her bedroom doorway, my hand running up the frame, above my head. She looked so beautiful, in a weird way. Her hair was fanned across her pillow, obscuring her face some, but shining in the sunlight pouring through the window. She had changed into a ribbed, white camisole and pink, flannel boxer shorts and she was sleeping on her side with the sheet tangled up between her legs. Her hands were pressed together, under her cheek, and the cami was askew, revealing some of her way-sexy stomach. Her tanned legs stretched out across the rumpled sheets like pulled caramel, and the curve of her hip was irresistible as her chest rose gently up and down in time with the pulse of bass from a nearby apartment.

And now, as the music beat next door, and I gazed on her sleeping form, I marveled over how little had changed. She was still the Chloe I used to know, too loving, too kind, hurt, vulnerable, and doing her damnedest not to let it show.

I never, for an instant, stopped loving her. Never. The past two plus years without her had been pure hell and my heart ached to straighten things out between the two of us, and to hold her again. Obviously, she was frightened. Afraid of getting hurt again. She needed me to take it slow, so I would take it slow. I could do that. Surely, I could do that. Couldn't I? With a sigh, I turned and tramped back into the living room.

When she came in later, I was sitting on her couch, sinking back into the cushions with my feet up on the trunk she used as a coffee table, reading the sports page. She inhaled shakily and I let the top of the page fold down so I could see her. She stood in the doorway of the living room with a hand held over her heart, and as I watched, she pushed her rumbled hair back in a way I found almost unbearably appealing. Her feet were bare except for her usual pink nail polish, and she had a very clean, natural look which I found immanently more attractive than her tailored business suits.

"You're here."

"Yes. I told you I would be. Did you think I would lie?"

She eyed me, but didn't say anything.

"Jack called earlier."

"You answered my phone?"

"I'm sorry," I interjected quickly. "It was reflex. The phone rang, and you were sleeping, and I dove to stop the noise, and then found I needed to say something to the person on the other end."

"What did you tell him?"

"I told him you were a 'bit under the weather' and you'd be taking the day off."

"Thanks," she said, relaxing a little.

"Then he asked why I was in your apartment."

"And you said...?"

"That it was none of his business."

"Ahh."

"At which point he said 'it damn well is my business, so what are you doing there?'"

"To which you replied...?"

"I told him I lied before, you weren't sick, you were tired, as we were up all night turning your bed into a three-ring circus and you were a little sore from—"

She held up her hands. "That's okay. I don't need to hear anymore."

An awkward pause descended while we stared at each other. "How are you feeling?" I asked her finally, folding up the paper and laying it aside.

"Miraculously better." Her smile melted my heart and I couldn't speak for a second. I picked up the half-finished crossword.

"I'm glad you're here. What's an eleven-letter word for "colluder?" It starts with a "c" and has an "n" as the third letter?" I patted the sofa beside me, clicking my pen and holding it at-the-ready. She grinned and did something totally unexpected; she ran over and leaped onto the couch beside me, bringing her head close to mine.

"Conspirator."

"Wow. You *must* be feeling better." I tried not to think about the way my heart beat faster simply having her closer, and the unbelievably good smell of her skin, still-warm from bed. "C-O-N-S-P-I-R-A-T-O-R." I scribbled the let-

ters down. "You were always better at this than I was. You think in Crossword."
We'd spent hours doing puzzles in our clubhouse of sorts. Her smile widened
even more.

"What else have you got?" She leaned a little closer to try to peer at the
clues, curling her legs up onto the couch. For a second I lost my composure.
Her bare arm brushed my forearm and her heat radiated all along my side as she
leaned into me. I cleared my throat.

"Well, let's see...gives us an "R" to start 12-across. 'A heavy gaseous radioac-
tive element.' Oh, radon."

"Radon," she guessed at the same time.

We laughed, and continued, for another fifteen minutes or so, to fill in the
ones I had left. When we were finished, I slapped the paper on the coffee table
with a satisfied snap. I shifted so I was turned toward her, my elbow resting on
the back of the couch. We had fallen so easily back into our normal camaraderie
for that space of time that I, without thought, reached over to play with her
hair. I tried to ignore the way she pulled back from me a fraction, her skin no
longer warming mine, but still only inches away.

She looked down, and then lifted her head to squint at me. "You haven't
asked me to talk about...anything."

By "anything" I knew she meant our messed-up relationship. "I'm willing to
table discussions of any serious subjects on one condition."

Her lips quirked into a smile, but she remained cautious. "What?"

"On the condition you spend the day with me, doing absolutely mindless
things."

Her smile wavered and her eyes swam with the pain she was trying so poor-
ly to hide. She got up and walked over to the window, crossing her arms in front
of her and staring silently out over the street below. I rose and followed, standing behind her and daring to reach around to touch her upper arms and whisper to her. "Please, Chloe...a few hours." She began to sway backward into my
arms, but then she stiffened.

"I don't know if I can do that." Her voice was strained.

"Just a few hours..." I murmured, my mouth near her ear. I let my eyes wan-
der over her profile hungrily. "That's all I'm asking." She turned in my arms and
I struggled to keep myself neutral, though being so close to her was completely
undoing me. Any emotion I would show would have her flying away from me,

like one of the little birds along the path in Central Park. My hands fell to her hips, and I kept them there loosely, keeping her close, but not trapping her.

"What would we do?" she asked, frowning. But the fact she asked meant she was considering it.

I scrambled for something. Remembering the image my mind captured seconds before, I offered, "Take a walk in Central Park, for starters."

She folded her arms, but didn't move away. "Walk in the park. Sounds like a great place to discuss things."

"Okay, a ride through the park then. We'll rent bikes." I gave her my best attempt at a winning smile. "Come on. You can't talk while riding bikes."

She still hesitated, breathing out shakily. After several seconds, her shoulders sank with discouragement and she asked, "What's the point, Nash?"

"No point," I reassured her. "Totally pointless. I just want to be with you." I made an attempt to keep the pleading out of my voice. "For old time's sake. I won't put any moves on you, I promise. No discussion more serious than 'which path do we take, left or right?'" I couldn't help but feel that was what we'd be truly doing, choosing what path to take. To the right, we stay together and build a future, to the left... I didn't want to think about the path on the left.

"Okay," she said finally.

"Okay?" I successfully kept a note of triumph out of my voice, although unable to keep my excitement from showing altogether. But instead of scaring her, it seemed to warm her.

"Okay," she repeated with a grin.

"Fantastic, then. We'll spend the day together, and then we'll have dinner," I added quickly.

"You're pushing it, Nabry." She narrowed her eyes. But I could still see the twinkle in them, something I hadn't seen since I found her again. And, I noted, she hadn't ruled out dinner either.

"Okay," I said happily, grabbing my jacket. "I'll go home and change, and be back in an hour. Will that give you enough time?"

"Plenty."

I came back and quickly kissed her on the forehead before she could think and then flew out the door feeling lighter than I had since things fell apart between us. Maybe, just maybe, we could make things work.

Chloe

I lathered soap over my body, feeling the last of the effects of the drugs Taylor gave me washing down the drain. I slowly became aware that I had been singing an old song, REO Speedwagon's, "I Can't Fight this Feeling," one of the songs on the radio the night I danced with Nash in the tree house. I couldn't even remember the last time I sang in the shower.

Get a grip. You know by now life isn't all sunshine and roses. I would spend the day with Nash, it would be pleasant, and then he would leave. I couldn't hope for more than that. Still, I found myself brooding over what to wear. The V-necked, black sweater? Too trashy. The Ranger's T-shirt? Not nearly trashy enough. What would Nash like? And why did that matter?

By the time he knocked on the door, I had a whole drawer-load of items strewn across my bed and abandoned on the floor.

"I can't find anything to wear," I blurted out when I answered the door. He looked cool and calm in a pair of faded-to-perfection jeans and a navy T-shirt which read, "Joe's Crab Shack."

"I can wait," he responded easily.

I went back to my bedroom, my heart going into panic mode, beating as fast as a hummingbird's. *I've got to find something.* I picked up a melon-colored, sleeveless sweater, and discarded it. *I can't keep him waiting. It's rude. What does one wear to bike in the park with your ex-boyfriend who you're still in love with but can't bear to be with and who dragged you out of the back seat of a cab and... did he carry me up the stairs?...and whom you did crossword puzzles with?*

I didn't seem to have anything in my closet suited for such an occasion. When I came out fifteen minutes later, my hair carefully done up in a banana clip to look carelessly done up, having chosen a tank top which was a confusion of purples and browns, tight, but not revealing, and a pair of denim shorts, he rose off the couch as if coming to attention. I loved the way he looked at me, as if in awe, but not like he wanted to jump my bones at the first opportunity. I hopped in the doorway, trying to pull the strap of my sandal up and noting how his eyes followed the gamut of my legs.

"I'm ready," I announced with a smile.

"Shall we?" he asked, offering me his elbow. I slipped my hand through it and couldn't help but give his arm a squeeze. It was strange how much it seemed like old times when we were together, like the two-plus years we were apart never happened. It was strange, and frightening, because I couldn't forget what happened. Those who forget the past are doomed to repeat it, right?

I was surprised to find he had the bikes waiting for us at the bottom of the stairs. He whipped out a five-dollar bill and handed it to a little, African-American boy who he must have paid to watch the bikes while he went upstairs to get me. The kid took off with a happy whoop. I noticed one of the bikes had a wicker basket attached to the back. I gestured to it. "What's that?"

"A picnic lunch."

"Picnics sound like places to talk."

He didn't comment, simply climbed on board the bike with the basket and held the other one up for me. I hesitated, with a faux frown, then smiled and boarded my bike as well.

It was a wonderful day, probably seventy-five, the sun burning strong, but a beautiful, gentle breeze licked at our hair and kept our skin cool. Before we knew it, we entered Central Park by the West End. Nash biked ahead, or fell back to comment on something, but kept things light as he promised.

Soon we entered the tear-shaped trail in a section of Central Park dedicated to the memory of John Lennon called Strawberry Fields. For as often as I had been to the park, I never made it to this section and found it to be quite stunning. I remembered John's widow, Yoko Ono, contributed a million dollars to its maintenance and improvements and it contained something like over one-hundred-twenty different species of plants and trees.

I watched Nash in front of me, moving with grace and effortlessness over the pathways. He still had the cutest butt, I couldn't help but notice. He came to a stop, and I almost rammed into him, I was so focused on watching his tight tush. He was straddling his bike and looking at a mosaic spread out in a circle before us. In the middle it read "Imagine," after Lennon's famous song, and someone had arranged pink and yellow roses in the form of a peace sign over the stones. Nash seemed lost in thought.

"What are you thinking about?"

He looked over at me. "I'd tell you, but I promised not to discuss serious stuff." He stepped on his pedals again and rode off. I hurried to follow him. What had the memorial to the martyred Beatle made Nash imagine?

We continued, passing by the Swedish cottage—where one of the only public marionette companies produced shows for New York audiences—through the Shakespeare Garden—which contained only plants mentioned in one of the Bard's plays—and on to the Jacqueline Kennedy Onassis Reservoir in the center of the park. After some time, Nash pulled over and I coasted up to a stop next to him.

"How are you doing?"

"Whoo," I panted. "Some of those hills are doozies. What do you have in here?" I laid my hand on the royal blue and black thermal cooler strapped to the back of my bike.

"Water." He smiled, clearly proud of himself.

"You thought of everything." I slid the zipper around its track and snatched a bottle out for each of us. I tossed one to him and he caught it with a grin.

"How about we make it to the other side of the reservoir, and then we'll eat lunch."

"You're calling the shots."

"And don't you forget it." He stepped on his pedal and turned it up a notch, challenging me a bit. I worked out at the gym five days a week, but it had been a while since I spent a whole morning biking. Still, I wasn't about to give him the satisfaction of besting me, so, despite my screaming thighs, I poured it on as well, sneaking up finally to pass him.

Changing positions in the lead like this frequently, we finally made it to the other end of the reservoir, huffing and puffing, biting back the side stitches which were squeezing us as the sweat rolled down our backs and between my breasts uncomfortably. But, it felt good. It felt good to challenge myself; it felt good to be with him.

He spread a blanket in the grass and unhooked the picnic basket, bringing it to the banks of the water where I had flopped wearily. I turned my head to look over at him, squinting one eye in the bright sun. "I hope you packed that thing full. I'm starving now."

"I don't think you'll be disappointed." He slowly slid out a bottle of wine and raised his eyebrows.

"Ooh. Gimme." I reached for the bottle. "You did pack a corkscrew, didn't—" but before I could even complete my thought, he handed me one.

"How could I have doubted you?" I fiddled with the bottle while he set everything else out, and then he came up behind me.

"Here," he murmured. "Let me help." He kneeled behind me, reaching around me to take hold of the corkscrew. Relinquishing control to him, I put my hands on the grass behind me, near his legs, squeezing the bottle between my bent knees to secure it. He was so close, like at the warehouse, but I wasn't as frightened anymore. He made a few adjustments, then, turned the screw a time or two before he began to work the arms down, guiding the cork out of the neck with a faint *pop*. He slid the bottle out from between my legs, and turned so he was by my side, facing me. He poured us each a glass of what turned out to be some kind of fabulous white wine, handed me mine, and clinked his against it, looking me intently in the eye for a long moment. Even before he spoke, he had my heart in my throat. "To new beginnings."

My throat seemed to temporarily close. He sipped his wine, watching me with a smile on his face. I choked some of mine down, and then took another long drink, nearly finishing off my glass. He placed a plate of crackers between us and a tub of...something.

"What is that?" I asked curiously.

"Ham pate."

"Did you make it?"

"Are you kidding?" He snorted. "There's this gourmet place down the block. I thought I'd give it a try. I hope it's good," he added, looking somewhat concerned now, after noticing its odd color and pungent scent.

"I'm sure it's delicious." I gamely spread some on a cracker, and tried it. It wasn't my favorite, very pickly. "It's...pretty good."

He read my face, and tried a bite of his own. He grabbed a napkin and spit it out. "That stuff is horrid."

I chuckled. "Yeah. It is pretty bad."

"Why didn't you say something?"

"I don't know. I thought maybe you'd like it." I averted my eyes and stifled my giggles.

"Like it?" he screamed in mock shock. "It tastes like what I imagine the stuff I clean out of my bathroom sink pipes taste like."

I laughed.

He plucked a grape from a vine on a plate in front of him and popped it into my mouth to silence me. "It's good to see you laugh," he said quietly, choosing another grape for himself.

I glanced down, at a loss for words.

He pretended not to notice. "Well, let's hope this cheese is better than that disgusting pate." He reached into the basket and plucked out a cheese wrapped in red wax, which turned out to be delicious. He also had strawberries and some out-of-this-world petit fours.

"Oh, my gosh. Those were so good. What's the name of that store again?"

"Dina's Fine Dining."

"Man. I've got to get those some time."

"Are you ready to get going again?"

"I better, or I'm gonna gain five pounds from all this wonderful food you brought." He began gathering things up, but I grabbed his arm. "Thank you, by the way, for everything. For taking care of me last night, for this wonderful picnic, for renting—"

"You're welcome," he answered simply.

We got on our bikes and followed the path through the north end of the park before heading back south and around the other side of the reservoir. We pedaled past the Metropolitan Museum of Art, and the Great Lawn. We saw Belvedere Castle, sitting high on the hill overlooking Central Park, with the Turtle Pond below. We stopped and admired the Alice and Wonderland statue and drank water, watching the children climb all over it, and commenting on how we would have loved to climb on it when we were kids. That naturally led into discussion of Nash's misadventure when he tried to jump the creek, which made us laugh so hard we were drawing looks from strangers.

Then we cut up and took a loop around the Ramble, easily the most beautiful area in all of Central Park. It was amazing. You would swear you were a million miles from civilization, when, in reality, not far away, the world's largest skyscrapers rose.

As we neared the South End of the park, we ran across the carousel, and I fell in love with it. The horses on the outer ring were nearly life-sized and carved and painted with such vivid reality it seemed you could almost feel their breath and hear their impatient snorts. We read a plaque about the history of the carousel which told us one had been there since 1871. As legend goes, the original was powered by a blind mule and a horse which walked a treadmill in an underground pit. The thought of these poor animals toiling to make their painted counterparts go around in an endless circle made me sad. Around the turn of the century, this carousel was replaced by a steam-powered version, but in 1924, it was destroyed by fire. A second fire in 1950 took out its replacement. Thus began an exhaustive search by the Parks Department which turned up the current ride, actually found abandoned in an old trolley terminal on Coney Island.

Seeing how drawn I was to it, Nash insisted we take a ride. He sat astride a white steed which was rearing, while I mounted a more subdued beauty with a brown coat and a rich, black mane. The pair was side-by-side, and stationary, but they seemed to be gazing at each other, Nash's looking at mine with fierce ardor, mine at his with candor and a sort of awe-struck reverence. Central Park danced around us to the music of the calliope and I felt, for a second, as if I was living in a fairy tale.

The air movement cooled down my face, warm from the sun and biking, and as I looked at Nash, I almost believed it could be true. Maybe he was my valiant prince in a shining suit of armor. Maybe it was possible to be happy in this world. But I knew hope could be a cruel thing, so I spoke severely to my heart while children laughed around us, and parents took pictures of them proudly. When the ride came to an end, Nash helped me down, grabbing my hips as I slid off the varnished surface of my horse. When my toes hit the ground, he was looking at me intently. His mount seemed to peer over his shoulder, his big, black eyes powerful and demanding. Before I could think, or feel, or move, Nash pressed his lips to mine. His kiss awakened in me dormant feelings I thought quenched forever and my lips responded automatically, craving him without relenting. His hands were behind my neck, tilting my lips up more so he could further pillage them, his thumbs brushing my cheeks softly. I opened my eyes slowly as he at last pulled back, almost afraid he would be gone, an imaginary lover, an imaginary Nash. But he remained with his hands behind my neck, his eyes as lost as mine to the reality of the moment, to people brushing past and parents 'tut-tutting' as they ushered their children around us.

"Chloe..." he murmured, his speech thick. "I..."

My heart went from zero to sixty in 1.2 seconds. I was more frightened than at any time Tate bullied me. I broke away from him in a panic and rushed forward, finding a break in the press of bodies and horses, and jumping to the ground. I passed through the throng of people waiting to board the ride, hopping a small wrought-iron fence which also held representations of horses on it. I ran a yard or two, but then stopped, asking myself why I ran in the first place. Nash was seconds behind me. He put a hand on my shoulder and turned me.

"I'm sorry."

"No, Nash. You shouldn't have to apologize for kissing someone. I'm..." I struggled for the right words, "...royally screwed up," I finished in disgust. "This has been great, it really has, but can we go home now? It's just...it's been a lot..."

"I know. I pushed you too hard too fast. Dammit. I was trying so hard not to."

Something about the way he said it struck me as funny. Impulsively, I grabbed his hand. "And you were doing a good job, too."

I could tell he was internally berating himself, but he stopped the second he registered my playful tone and looked at me, breaking into a smile.

I looked at his hand, so wonderfully familiar. I had seen it grasping his bike's handle bars, seen it clutching the steering wheel of his old, blue truck, seen the way it traversed over my body in a seedy hotel room...

"I'm the one who should be sorry. I'm the one who is messed up."

He shook his head. "You can't take all the responsibility for this, Clo. I've had my hand in it, too."

We paused, unsure of how to continue. "Can we finish our ride back home so I can shower before you take me out somewhere fabulous for dinner?"

You would have thought I handed him the Nobel Prize. "Sure. Sure." He subtly took my hand and folded it over his arm, turning in the direction we left our bikes. "And I'll go back to my place and get changed, too. We have reservations at seven."

"Reservations? Weren't you getting a little ahead of yourself, Nabry? I hadn't even agreed to dinner yet."

"Ahh," he replied with a wave of his hand. "I knew I'd charm the pants off you."

"Really?" I responded with a laugh.

He stopped at the boundary of the carousel marked by the chains. "Seriously. I'll try to behave myself tonight. Keep these lips in check." He tapped them with his index finger.

We stepped over the chains.

"Nash...?"

"Hmm..."

I leaned over to whisper in his ear. "Don't try too hard." I released his arm and took up my bike, racing off before he could respond.

CHAPTER TWELVE

Nash

I stood outside her doorway, and guess who pops his head out? The Latino guy. This time I'm standing there in dress pants and a nicer shirt with a bouquet of flowers. He laughed and shook his head, saying something in Spanish—I think I recognized the word "loco"—and went back in. Then Chloe opened the door and I was blown away. She had on this killer dress, kind of like a zebra pattern, but it veed down almost to wear she wore a wide black belt. Her hair was curly and up and she looked so good I was literally speechless.

"Nash, is something wrong?"

I breathed out. "No. No. It's just...wow, that dress."

She looked down, trying to draw the crisscross material of the top of the dress closer so it covered more. "It's too much, isn't it? I'll go change."

I grabbed her arm. "Wait, wait, wait. It's not that. Not that at all." I bent and quickly kissed the corner of her lips before she could move away. "I was sort of...stunned. You look so incredible."

She blushed, and seemed flustered. "Oh. Okay. Good. Thanks." She didn't look at me, grabbing her purse and a filmy black shawl from a table near the door. I didn't move as she tried to pass me through the door. She looked up.

I touched her face lightly. "You okay?"

She smiled. "Yeah." But she looked down again and then glanced sideways, avoiding eye contact.

I put a fist under her chin and lifted her face. "Surely you're used to being complimented like that."

She shuffled her feet. "Well...yeah, sort of." She finally looked me in the eyes. "But not by you." She bit her lip, perhaps afraid she'd revealed too much.

I let my hand brush the skin of her neck, and out toward her shoulders, my eyes following the graceful curves. Her breath quickened and she quivered as I said, my voice sounding husky, "Well, we'll have to change that." I brought the flowers up to hand them to her.

"Oh, Nash. They're beautiful. Let me put them in water really quick."

She returned after a minute or two and I moved so she could exit, dropping my hand to her back to escort her, where I discovered the oval of bare-skin her dress didn't cover.

She locked the door behind her, and we hastened down the stairs. When we got to the truck, I opened the door for her, feeling a little bit embarrassed by my sad little chariot. But when I got to the other side and slid in, Chloe was running her hands over the dashboard lovingly.

"I can't believe you still have this old thing." Her eyes shone as she looked at me. "We had a lot of fun in this truck."

I chuckled. "Yes, we did." I started the engine, and she skootched beside me, like she had in the old days. For a minute, it was easy to forget how much time had passed, and how much things had changed. But as I looked at her out of the corner of my eye, it struck me; she wasn't the girl I knew before. Her moment of nostalgia over, she glanced around the cab and out to the street, her foot tapping against the hard plastic of the dash. Instead of being the one to comfort her, I was the one who made her unnerved, and knowing that hurt. Maybe we couldn't get around this, maybe you only got one shot, and I messed it up somehow. I stopped at a light and turned to look at her, but she was gazing out the window, oblivious. That phrase, "You can't go home again," played in my head, and a sadness seeped into my soul.

We got to the little Italian restaurant I chose, mere blocks from my place.

As we approached a voice called out. "Nash. How are you? It is Tuesday night, isn't it? But tonight you have a beautiful woman with you." Adolpho took Chloe's hand and gave it a smarmy kiss, his gaze caressing her without even the slightest bit of subtlety, his pearly-white teeth sparkled out of his olive-toned face and he suddenly reminded me of a shark.

"Save your charm. She's with me," I said while passing him.

"Ahh...but that's no guarantee, is it?" he returned, low enough so Chloe wouldn't hear him.

I shot him a dark look.

"You eat here every Tuesday?" Chloe asked out of the upturned corner of her mouth.

I shrugged. "I'm not a very good cook."

"But pasta's probably one of the easiest things to cook."

"So they tell me," I returned with a grunt.

Adolpho brought us to a semi-circular booth, again flirting with Chloe in an overbearing, European way, and we each ended up sitting at one end of the booth, with miles of empty vinyl bench between us. We ordered, and talked pleasantly about my artwork, until the wine came. She took her glass right away and drifted back into silence. I took a long, slow drink of my wine, studying her over the rim of my glass, then, set it on the table, stretching my hands out in a relaxed pose behind the booth. "We're going to have to talk about it eventually."

Her gaze darted to mine, with a hint of anger. "I know." She took a drink of her own wine. "What do you want to know?"

Her response surprised me. "You're ready to talk?"

She nodded, her gaze focused on the candle in the middle of the table.

"Okay." I thought about my question carefully. I wanted to work her into things gently. "How long have you been doing real estate?"

She looked up at me with a small smile. Perhaps she could tell what I was doing. "It will be three years in June."

I thought about this, letting a silence settle over the table. That was pretty close to the last time I'd seen her, but there was still a gap of several months. I drank again leisurely, contemplating my next line of attack, but as I did so, the food arrived. Although I was usually thrilled by Davenucci's fast service, this time I cursed them silently. We ate, and made small talk about how good the food was and the restaurant's décor, and even Adolpho, but we never got back to the subject of why we fell apart.

When the table was cleared, I looked at her again. She gazed back, her face tense, probably sensing the shift in conversation. Before anything else interrupted us, I needed to get down to the bottom of things. "Why did you leave?"

She looked a little shaken, not expecting the direct approach. When she spoke it was barely above a whisper. "Because he came back."

Chloe

The look on Nash's face was indescribable when I told him Tate came back. I could barely get the words out of my mouth; I was still so horrified by them.

About three weeks after my hospital visit, I walked next door to find Nash's mom babbling incoherently. By the time Nash's brother, Ed, got there, the EMTs pretty much decided she'd suffered a massive stroke. Nash came home for a couple of days, and, together, the three sons put her into a nursing home.

It was terribly hard on Nash. Without a dad around when he was growing up, his mom was everything to him.

Nash missed even more class time when he came home to help his mom, so I chalked it up to that when he didn't call, even though it made me feel so alone. With Mrs. Nabry gone, there was no one within miles of my place. I dreaded coming home to an empty house and spaghetti-Os night after night, and a too silent phone.

A week after that, I was in the shower when, suddenly, Tate was there.

I had spent the entire afternoon restocking shelves in the local grocery market where I had a job. My skin was coated in a layer of dried sweat, and my muscles were groaning, so the hot water felt amazing. I finished and turned the water off, dreaming of hopping in bed. When I drew the shower curtain back, Tate was there, sitting on the toilet. I screamed and tugged the curtain back in place.

"Hello, Chloe-girl. Long time no see."

His grating voice sent a shiver up my spine which had nothing to do with me being cold. I peeked out. He had taken the towels off the rack, so I had nothing to wrap around me. It enraged me. How dare he come in my bathroom while I was showering and then wait to gawk at me. I snatched the shower curtain from the rod and wrapped it around me, stepping out onto the bathmat in as dignified a manner as I could summon in the situation.

But having his little peep-show thwarted infuriated him. Before I could reach the door, he grabbed me around the middle and dragged me back into the center of the room. Tate was a big man, and his years at the mill made him unbelievably strong. I kicked and flailed but he subdued me with what seemed like very little effort on his part.

"Where do you think you're going now, sister?" He pressed me up against the closet door roughly, keeping me in place with his body. The curtain was still between us, but my body was bare where I was smashed against the door. Then, the hiss of leather being pulled through a buckle, along with the clanking of the metal parts, told me he was messing with his belt. At first I thought he was going to beat me with it. Then I was afraid he was undoing his pants to rape me. He looped his belt around the shower rod, which was built into the wall. I concluded he intended to hang me somehow from the piece of piping, and I began to fight even more frantically.

"Stop it, Chloe. Now be still." He spun me around and cracked me across the face, hard, and I stumbled, whacking my head solidly on the edge of the tub on my way to the cold, hard tile. He grabbed my arm, nearly jerking it out of its socket as he hauled me again to my feet, a little dazed, and standing completely nude. He stuck my hands through the loop he created with his belt and pulled until my wrists were held tightly against the cold metal shower rod. The edges of the belt cut into my wrists, but I was trying to twist and see what Tate was doing, if only in the mirror. I caught my image in the still partially steamed mirror, strung up like a side of cattle, naked and bleeding from my head and mouth, with a look of sheer terror in my eyes, totally exposed and totally alone.

He sat back on the toilet. "There now. You sit and listen to what I've got to say." I could tell by the way his eyes were squinty and unfocused, and his tongue loose and unwieldy in his mouth, he was trashed.

"Tate, you better get out of here before Nash returns," I bluffed.

"Ahh." He sat forward, a gleam coming into his eyes. "Exactly the subject I wanted to talk about." He slapped his knee. Then his demeanor turned cold, he stood and walked over to me, pinching my chin in his hand. "Don't you lie to me, Chloe-girl. You and me both know that good-for-nothing boyfriend of yours is not here. He's got himself someone else. I've seen him."

A pain shot through me. "I don't believe you. You tried to make me believe that before."

"I thought you'd say that." His hand rummaged clumsily in his inner coat pocket to slide out some five by seven pictures of Nash, his arms around a pretty blonde, taken from different angles, one where they were kissing. "This is why he hasn't been around. He's done with you, now Clo. He's got him somethin' better. Yep. Moved on." Tate dropped the pictures and they fluttered down onto the sunny, yellow bath mat. I twisted my head, straining to stare at them. The pain stabbed into my heart so deeply I felt nauseous.

Tate let his eyes roam over my body and a seething rage filled me. Without even really thinking, I reached and grabbed onto the curtain rod, lifting my feet and kicking Tate in the chest as hard as I could. His body flew across the room, hitting the toilet. He rolled over, fell to the floor and lay still.

I stood shivering, the now-cold water from my hair running down my back, adding to the chill. It was perfectly quiet except for the *drip, drip* of the faucet I hadn't gotten turned off all the way. I knew I might only have minutes before Tate might be up and at me again. I worked to release my wrists from the belt, my gaze flying back and forth between what I was doing, and his body. He moaned once, and shook his head back and forth, but he didn't rise. The belt was cinched so tightly I had difficulty releasing it, and the harder I tugged at it, the more it cut into me. I sobbed, trying to work more quickly. It seemed to take forever, but I finally got it off.

Tate lay between me and the door. At my feet were the pictures of Nash and the blonde. I wanted to pick them up, to study them, to find a way to disprove what Tate said. But his words came ringing back to me. Nash hadn't called me in days. But I couldn't think about that now, I had to get out. Still, I grabbed a picture from off the floor and pressed it to my chest.

I approached Tate cautiously, my heart in my throat, every second expecting him to wake up and grab me like the bad guy in some horror movie; I was in the bathroom after all. There was no blood anywhere around him, so I began to suspect he may be faking, and the only way out lie just beyond his left shoulder. I held my breath and inched closer. His chest was rising and falling evenly. I lifted my leg, finally, to step over his prone body.

To my relief, he never moved more than to moan and move his head a little. Once on the other side of the door, I didn't look back. I grabbed some clothes off the dresser, and didn't even take the time to put them on until I was deep in the woods, panting after having run so far.

I leaned back against a tree trunk, yanking my jeans up and wondering for the first time where I was running to. I knew what I was running from, I would never again return to that house. But where to go? I pulled out the picture of Nash and soaked in every detail, his hand on her shoulder, her smile, electric, the look in his eyes, as if he was gazing on his heart's treasure. I shut my eyes, squeezing out a tear which trickled down my face. My heart was in a vise. Ripping the picture in two, I dropped it on the forest floor. Sobs, which had been rising inside me since Tate's voice first ripped through me, destroyed me completely.

When the sun rose, I woke up lying in the mud, cold and sore. I sat, stiff, moving my jaw experimentally. The pain roared through me, making me cry out. My head was throbbing, my throat ached from my fierce weeping of the night before, and I was left with the same question...where to go?

CHAPTER THIRTEEN

Nash

My stomach dropped out when she told me Tate had returned. It took me a few moments to regain my capacity for speech. I shook my head back and forth slowly. "He...didn't..."

Anticipating my question, she shook her head. "Not like the last time."

I nodded, relieved. But, when I looked at her again, and noticed how pale she had become, even in the candlelight, I knew there was more to this story. She brought her napkin up to wipe her mouth and I noticed her hands were shaking. I closed my eyes. This was all my fault. If I hadn't gotten so wrapped up in my studies... I should have asked her to live with me in the city after we took Mom to the nursing home. I shouldn't have left her alone to be preyed upon by that monster.

"Nash, can we get some air?"

"Sure." I paid the waiter, and we left the restaurant. Out of habit, I began to walk toward home, my hand over her shoulder. I looked down at her. "Better?" She nodded. It had turned chillier while we were inside, so I pulled her closer to my side, and she seemed to naturally mold to me. We walked half of a block in silence. "So, what did he do to you?" I asked finally. She swallowed.

"I had gotten a job at Shiny's, stocking shelves and checking people out. One night I came home...I was tired, and sweaty, so I hopped in the shower, and... Tate came in. I didn't hear him until I turned the water off."

I imagined him, sitting and waiting for her, getting off on the idea she was naked behind the curtain and not even aware of his closeness. We had stopped walking, and turned toward each other. The streetlight illuminated her face, but she was lost to the memory.

"He had...taken the towels. So I ripped the curtain down and draped it around me."

Good for you. I could almost see the rebellious tilt of her chin.

"But he was strong. He was always so strong." Her voice became hollow. "He strung me up, with his belt, to the shower rod."

My jaw tightened. "Did he...touch you?"

"I didn't give him the chance. I kicked him in the gut and he fell against the toilet and either hit his head on the wall, or passed out from his drinking. I didn't stick around to find out." She turned and started walking again, and I hurried to catch up to her.

"So you...found a place of your own? A place where Tate couldn't find you?" She looked off to one side, tears mounting in her eyes.

"I had to get away."

"Why didn't you call me?"

Her face began to crumble, but then she took a shaky breath. "Not here. Not now."

"We're not far from my place," I said hurriedly. Now I had her talking, I didn't want her to stop. She nodded and started walking a little faster. Our minds were so occupied with the past, we didn't see them, but two big guys stepped into our path. We moved to go around them, and they moved as well, blocking our path again. I raised my head and really looked at them. They both wore grey sweat jackets, with the hoods pulled up. I realized the street was darker than usual, a light was out. That was something, as a New Yorker, I should have noticed as we were walking, but I was too preoccupied with her story.

"Hey. How's it goin'?" one asked in a deep voice. The other chuckled low and menacingly.

Then Chloe was jerked from my arms from behind. I spun and two more stood, in black hoodies, and one had his forearm across Chloe's neck.

"Let's take our business into the alley, shall we?" the first one said mockingly. When I hesitated, he added, "If you don't want your little girlfriend here hurt, do as we tell you." I had no choice, so our little party shuffled into the alley, one of the guys hanging back, to guard the entrance, looking up and down the street.

I faced the speaker and wordlessly surrendered my wallet, not dreaming of fighting them with Chloe in their grasp. Chloe made a little squeak, and I twisted my head in her direction. The thug holding her had his face buried in her hair, saying something into her ear. Chloe's eyes were closed, and she was straining her neck away from him. "No," she breathed in response to something he said, her voice sounding desperate.

I could hear him now, his voice low and lusty. "Come on, baby. Don't you want—" The guy didn't have time to complete his thought because I sprang at him, catching him by surprise. Chloe screamed as I was dragged off him. I hadn't had enough time to inflict any real damage. Somebody punched me in the face, another landed a blow to my solar plexus, doubling me over and knocking the wind out of me.

"Get her stuff," the first one barked, grabbing one of my arms as his partner secured the other.

"Oom...yeah. I'd like to get her stuff."

I lifted my head, gasping for air, and his meaty hands were rubbing up and down her bare arms. She seemed to be folding herself inward, like a collapsing umbrella.

"Huh, baby?" He lowered his head to her neck to taste her skin.

"Get her stuff," one of the two holding my arms, who seemed to be the leader, bellowed again.

The hulk who had Chloe glared at his friend from underneath his hood. "Give me your ring, honey." The only ring Chloe wore was the wedding set her father gave to her mother. I knew it was one of the few things she had left to remember them by. It sparkled in a shaft of light coming from the far end of the ally as she tried to comply, but her shaking hands made it difficult for her to remove it. "Come on," he screamed, pulling her back again against his chest with a thud. She finally wrestled it off her finger and dropped it into the waiting hands of the man across from her.

"The necklace," he reminded his accomplice, who then brought his hands up to mess with the chain around Chloe's neck. His thick fingers couldn't manage the clasp, so he pushed her away from him into the middle of the ally.

"Take it off," he growled. She brought her hands up to the back of her neck. "Take it all off, baby," he added, his eyes glowing in the dark circle of his hood. They all laughed, except the leader guy, who seemed to be getting impatient. The necklace finally fell from her neck and she handed it over. She just wanted the ordeal to end, I could tell.

While she was distracted with giving the leader her necklace, the brute who was bothering her grabbed her and threw her up against the wall, still pressing a forearm against her chest. I strained forward, but could not break free, my heart aching for her. From my angle I could see her profile, and she looked kind of shell-shocked.

"You sure are a looker," the big mugger muttered with an air of disappoint-ment, using his free hand to adjust his crotch, tight from his excitement. He reached down below the hem of her dress and ran his hand up the back of her thigh, lifting her dress up nearly to her hip and squeezing her flesh, grunting, and pushing his pelvis against her.

I went berserk. I freed a hand and coldcocked the guy next to me, who went down to his knees. I shook off the other guy and almost reached the thug with Chloe when his partner grabbed me and slammed me, face-first, into the brick building, right next to Chloe. I looked at her, my face still fierce, hers hor-rorstricken, inches away from mine.

The lookout guy behind me had my arm twisted, and put enough pressure on it to make me wince. "Let's get out of here." With a final shove, they released us and took off in a pack down the alley.

"Look me up sometime, gorgeous," Chloe's tormentor called, his voice echoing along the alley walls.

"Shut up, you ass," the leader shouted. They all boarded motorcycles parked on the opposite street and roared away.

Chloe clutched at me. "Oh, my Lord! Nash!"

I was still having trouble catching my breath, and was a little worse for wear. "I'm okay." I pulled her into my arms. "I'm sorry, Chloe."

"Don't be silly. This wasn't your fault."

"But I should have protected you." *I should have now, and I should have then.* My guilt threatened to suffocate me.

"There were *four* of them. You're not Chuck Norris. You can't be expected to—"

"Still."

She pushed some hair back on my forehead to examine a cut made by the brick. I held her fiercely to me by the hips. She smiled. "You did inflict some damage."

"Not enough," I grumped, but then groaned a little at a stabbing pain in my rib cage.

"Let's get you home," she said worriedly, but she didn't move, continuing to brush the hair from my face. She pressed her lips lightly to the uninjured side of my mouth. She pulled back, and then looked at me again, with a strange ex-pression on her face. I was too stunned to speak. She brought a finger up and traced my lips, hopping over the cut part, and then slowly moved in again. I closed my eyes, savoring the sensation of her lips on mine. I clutched at her, and took control of the kiss, ignoring the pain where it was tender and tasting her greedily. When she finally pulled away, her lips turned up at the corners a little, although something about her demeanor still made her seem wary of me. "We should probably get going. It's not safe around here, you know," she joked with a shaky smile.

I grinned, still kind of rocked by her kiss.

I limped along next to her silently, nursing my bruised ego, and directed her to my place. By the time we got there, my gut was feeling a ton better, and my lip had pretty much stopped bleeding. But she cried out when she got a look at me in the full light of my apartment.

"Oh, Nash. Sit down. Let me get you some ice for that lip."

I did flop on the couch, but begged her, "I'm sure I look worse than I feel. Don't baby me." She came back with ice wrapped in a towel and curled up beside me, applying it gingerly to my lip. "You're making me feel like crap," I muttered against the towel, although the ice actually felt awesome.

She pulled it away, her eyes wide. "Why?"

Although I wanted nothing more than to stay next to her, I jumped from the couch, and went over to the little, narrow window by my door, which was so dirty on the outside you couldn't see through it anyway. "Oh, come on, Clo. I've never been able to protect you, and you know it." I spun around. "That's why you didn't call me when Tate came back, isn't it?"

She paled, but answered readily. "No. No. That's not it at all."

"Then...why? Why didn't you call me?" I couldn't keep the hurt out of my voice.

She looked away, tears springing to her eyes. After a moment she gazed at me with a sense of determination. "Because Tate..." Her voice became choked, and she had to start again. "Because Tate told me about you and your girlfriend. I didn't want to bother you with my problems since you found someone new."

"*Bother* me with your problems? What the hell are you talking about, Chloe?" I yelled. "And, what girlfriend? I was in love with you." She shut her mouth and stared at me, her face tight. I ground my teeth together and had to glance away for a second. "And you bought his line of bullshit?"

"*He had pictures*!" she screamed at me hysterically. "He had pictures," she re-peated quietly, then covered her face with her hands and cried.

Like a flash of lightning I saw it, and it all made sense now.

Not long after Tate disappeared and I went back to New York for school, I spotted him. It was a beautiful day, and I was studying for my art history exam, sitting on a brick post at the bottom of a short set of stairs along one of the walkways which led from one of the classroom buildings.

A shadow covered my page and a familiar voice called out, "Why, if it isn't Nash Nabry?"

I looked up to see Molly Sherandon standing above me. Molly used to date my brother, Ed. It was so good to see a face from home, I admit it, I threw my arms around her and swung her around in a circle as she laughed.

She gave me a quick peck on the lips. "It's so good to see you."

"You, too, Molly. How's that fiancé of yours?"

"You mean, husband?" She stuck out her hand to show me the mega-rock on her finger. "I'm married now," she squealed.

"No, kidding? Congratulations." I hugged her again and then got that feel-ing I was being watched. I looked up and caught sight of Tate beyond her, hand-ing a camera, and some money to some tourist kid, and receiving a roll of film in exchange. I never thought much about it, I was too astonished to see him. I mean, in the whole wide city of New York, when we'd been searching high and low for him at home, he shows up a few feet from me? I ran after him, but a bell had rung and students were spilling out of the buildings in the bright sunshine. I lost him in a crowd.

So, he took pictures of me to bring back to Chloe. He knew he could play off the insecurities he had put in place inside of her. I walked over to the couch slowly and knelt in front of her.

"Oh, Chloe," I murmured, finding it was all I could say as the pieces clicked together in my mind. "So you didn't call because you thought... There was no other woman."

"There's no need to deny it now. You weren't calling, you weren't writing..."

A stab of pain pieced my heart. I gulped. "Yes. You are right. I stopped call-ing and writing because I got caught up in my work." I looked into her face. "I know how stupid that was. To ever let anything come between us. But I did try to get you a couple of times, I guess our schedules didn't jibe."

"Then who was the pretty blonde, Nash?" she spat. "Who was the pretty blonde in the photos Tate splashed across my bathmat that night?"

"Molly Sherandon."

"Molly...you mean Billy Sherandon's sister?"

I nodded. "She went out with Ed, and I ran into her on campus one day, and we talked all about her new husband and their honeymoon to Key West."

She stared at me blankly a moment, tears still rolling down her face. "You told me once Ed went out with Billy's kid sister."

"Yeah," I nodded, smiling. "She was over at our house all the time. She was like a big sister. More like a mother, actually. She was very bossy."

"So you and she never...?"

"No. Are you kidding? Ed would have killed me. He still had a thing for her."

She brought her hands together in her lap. "And I believed Tate." Her voice sounded dead.

I pushed the hair back from her face. "But it's okay. I understand now. He was playing you."

She sprang up, her voice rising. "But I shouldn't have believed him. You had never done an unkind thing to anyone. I should have known you would have called me first."

I stood, too, grabbing her shoulders, excited we would finally have this thing behind us. "But it doesn't matter, because it's all in the past. That's over now. We can start over."

She broke away from me, stumbling back a few feet and throwing her arm down to right herself on the coffee table, shaking her head. "No. You don't understand."

"Of course I understand. I understand you better than anyone."

"No, you don't," she rasped out, looking stricken. "You don't know what I've done. Or who I am now."

"It doesn't matter," I insisted. "It's in the past." I moved toward her and she backed up again.

"No, Nash. You don't know." She was sobbing now. "I threw everything we had away...on the word of a liar. I can't stay here anymore."

She bolted around the back of the couch for the door, but I dove to catch her arm.

"You're not going, Chloe."

She fought me. "Yes, I am."

"Chloe," I paused. "I just got the shit kicked out of me, but I swear, if you go out there, I'll drag you back here bodily."

She turned on me like a wildcat. "Nash!" she screamed, the sound piercing me. "Don't you get it? If you knew what I'd done, you would be throwing me out of here bodily."

"I don't believe that."

"*You don't know!*" she cried, her eyes blazing.

"Then tell me." I touched the side of her face. "Just tell me," I begged softly. She bit her lip, looking like she was considering it. "If I do..." Her voice became small, "You'll never look at me the same way again."

What had she done? A thought crossed my mind. Had she killed Tate Rodgers that night and then gone on the run? Didn't she know I would applaud her if she had? Was that what was haunting her?

"Okay." She took a deep breath. "I'll tell you."

CHAPTER FOURTEEN

Chloe

I loved him desperately still. How would I ever find the strength to tell him? I wished I had made it out the door. I could have run after those muggers and said, "Here I am. Use me up, then, shoot me dead. It's what I deserve."

And now, to be sitting across the couch from him, knowing he hadn't betrayed me at all, but I betrayed him. It was killing me. But I owed him an explanation. I owed him that, at least.

"Nash," I said weakly. He waited, never taking his gaze from me. "Could you..." I froze.

"Could I what?"

I swallowed, closing my eyes. "Could you kiss me one more time, for old time's sake, before I leave?"

"I'm not planning on your leaving," he said distinctly. He put his hand behind my hair, lifting it from my shoulder and caressing the nape of my neck. "But I will kiss you." He leaned in, brushing his lips across mine experimentally, and then taking me down on a long, sliding, breathless kiss.

When I opened my eyes, my head was spinning. I steeled myself. I had to get this over with.

"Like I told you, I knocked Tate out. I ran from of the house. I was so scared. I didn't stop until I was deep in the woods, and then I pulled my clothes on." I shivered, remembering the rough bark of the tree, as I leaned against it, naked and out of breath, my feet freezing from the cold mud. "I fell asleep on the ground, and when I woke up, I had to decide what to do." I turned to look at him, my heart heavy. "I couldn't go back. And I thought..." The pain struck me anew, and I had to take another breath. "I thought you didn't care anymore." He grabbed my hands and held them in his, both of us leaning forward on the edge of the couch, his knee touching mine. I closed my eyes, dreading telling him. "I didn't have anywhere else to go." I opened my eyes and gazed into his, seeking forgiveness even before confessing. "Ralph Denegan told me, if I ever needed something..." My voice faded out and I stared back over the years. Nash's voice called me back.

"The mechanic?"

I nodded. "I hiked into town. He took me to his cabin by the lake. At first, he was really nice to me. He took care of me. Fed me. He wouldn't let me get a job, said I needed to stay hidden, in case Tate came around. But I think now, he wanted me to become dependent on him."

"Then one night, he'd had a few, and he insisted I have some, too. I'd never really had anything to drink before, so I got a little tipsy. And then...he told me I owed him, that he loved me, he would always take care of me, and he took my clothes off." Nash paled, and I knew I needed to say the rest as fast as I could, before I chickened out. "He kissed me and told me to kneel. He unzipped his pants. He told me I couldn't get pregnant if I..."

Nash nodded, but looked away from me, and I knew that was it. He'd never look at me the same way again. I continued lifelessly.

"I hated it. Pretty soon he wanted it all the time. He'd come home for lunch, wake me up at night, pleading with me. One night, he bought me a dress, told me he was taking me out to a fancy dinner. But when we got to the restaurant, he pushed me down between his legs in the parking lot. When he was done, he drove me home without even taking me in to eat." I never told anyone about what happened between Ralph and I, and it felt good, in a sense, to unburden myself. My thoughts drifted. "Sometimes he would press me, with my stomach against the wall of the cabin, and grind on me and moan, telling me over and over again how hot I was, and what a good screw I would be. And, while it grossed me out for the most part..." I hesitated, finding the words to describe my emotions from that time difficult, and afraid to add anything more to the negative way Nash would view me now.

He squeezed my hand. "Go on, Clo. It's okay."

I looked at him for a second, wondering what must be going through his head. "Sometimes, I have to admit, as pathetic as this sounds, it made me feel good. Made me feel wanted. Made me feel loved. I know how wrong that is."

He shook his head. "I'm not judging you. Is there more you wanted to tell me?"

I thought about it, and the words continued to flow forth. Like a bottle of soda that's been shaken, it seemed to fizz out everywhere. "Once, when he was really drunk, he bent me over the footboard of the bed. Said it was better that way, I wouldn't get pregnant." I cringed, remembering how painful it was. "I ran away the next day, but he caught me. Begged me to stay. Told me he'd stay away from me if I came back. I had no money, so I really had no choice. But I started taking money from his wallet. A little at a time, so he wouldn't notice. And I saved. And he did stay away from me...for four or five days. After a while, he started begging me, telling me how beautiful I was and how good I was at it."

"Then, one night, he came home with a fifth of rum and a friend. They kept telling stories, laughing, and filling my cup. The stories kept getting cruder, and then, all of a sudden, the guy climbed on top of me and started unbuttoning my shirt while Ralph watched, with his hand down his pants. I flipped out. I bucked him off then started screaming and throwing things. I thought, for a moment, I truly lost my mind. Ralph got a little freaked out by it and sent his friend away, telling him, 'maybe today wasn't the day.'"

"When the guy left, Ralph laid into me. He never actually hit me, but he yelled at me, telling me I was ungrateful, after all he did for me, and he broke things. Then he coerced me, telling me maybe I wasn't ready for two at a time, but the least I could do after 'throwing my little fit' was to go down on his friend. He drove me into town, to this guy's place, but I refused to go in. He tried to drag me in, but I planted my feet on either side of the door frame and he finally gave up. When we got home, he told me to relax, everything would be okay, and kept giving me more rum. I finally passed out, sort of, but I could still hear his voice on the phone. 'Come on over now. She's ready for it. Believe me, Tommy, this is a night none of us is going to forget.' I struggled to pull myself off the couch, hearing his laughter echoing strangely in my ears, and feeling like I was working my way through salt water taffy. I managed to scramble out the door and stumble down to the lake. It's a wonder I didn't drown myself in my condition. I made it to town and took a bus. Made it all the way to New York. I had some money, but not enough. I met a guy on the bus, Mitch, the Plumber, I liked to call him. I don't even remember his last name. I lived with him until I got a job at McCummins Realty and had enough money for a place of my own.
"

Several seconds of silence passed. I gazed into his stunned face, the face I loved so much. "So, Nash. Still think you know me?" I was incredibly tired. He didn't respond. I stood and headed toward the door. At first, he didn't even turn. But when I opened the door, he rushed forward.

"No, wait. Don't leave." He pulled me back inside and into his arms, laying his cheek on top of my head. "I'm sorry," he whispered.

I squirmed, trying to pull away, not wanting to soil him with my past. "What for?" I balked.

"For what happened to you."

I gaped, astounded. "It didn't happen to me, Nash. I made choices."

"You made the best choices you could from a myriad of bad choices presented to you."

"That doesn't change the fact..." I drew a breath, then released it. Why didn't he understand? "I did things, Nash. It didn't stop there, you know. Once I had the power to please, it didn't stop with Mitch the Plumber. There was Max, the Horny Guy on the Corner, I'm not sure what he did for a living. And Bart of the Bad Breath. Do you need to hear the whole litany?" He shook his head and tried to interrupt me. I pushed away from him, pacing maniacally. "I didn't have intercourse with a one of them, but I got them off. Want me to list the ways how? In what places? In what positions?" He reached to pull me back into his arms. "Don't touch me!" I screamed hysterically. "I'm not the girl you fell in love with. She died in a cabin beside a lake when the oily hands of a mechanic first felt her up."

"Stop!" he screamed finally. "Stop! None of that matters. I love you."

I stared at him, dumbfounded. "Have you not been listening to a word I've said?"

"No. No, I've been listening. Believe me, I've been listening."

"Well, then, you—"

"Shut up!" he raged, and I clamped my mouth closed. I'd never seen him like this. "It's my turn to talk." He exhaled, but then picked up my pacing, walking back and forth in front of me with his hands on his hips. "I've been listening...to how man after man took advantage of you. Do I wish it hadn't happened? Sure. But does it change the fact I love you? Not one little bit."

"You're insane."

"Yeah, maybe so," he snapped. "But you're wrong when you say the girl I fell in love with is gone." He came to me and framed my face between his two hands. "I saw her take a ride with me through Central Park today and laugh at the kids climbing the Alice in Wonderland statue." His voice became soft, and he took me again into his arms. Although I wanted to pull away, I went into an automatic-melt mode he always inspired. "I saw her in the dreamy way you looked at that warehouse, like you could see all the potential there for something marvelous. I felt her there," he said, moving a strand of hair from my face and gazing into my eyes, "when you kissed me a little while ago."

My throat felt strangled. This couldn't be happening. How could he accept me knowing...? He just didn't understand. "That wasn't her. The girl you kissed, sh-she's...been taught. She knows how to kiss to fool men into thinking—"

He stopped me with his mouth, swallowing my protests with his kiss. "Chloe..." he murmured between kisses, a hint of desperation in his tone. "This is who you are. The girl you are with me."

I wanted so badly to believe him. He backed me up against the door and stopped his frantic movements to look at me with an intensity I had never seen before. "Don't let them win. Don't let them beat you down. I know you have love in your heart for me. I've seen it."

"I do. But...don't you understand? It's too late."

"Why, dammit? Because you being with a lot of men changed you? Well, maybe you being with one man will change you back, make things right. Please don't give up on us. Let me love you the way you should be loved."

Who could argue with that? I searched his eyes. Was it too much to hope for, that things could go back to the way they were for us? Things seemed so right, so natural since he'd shown up at my table at the restaurant yesterday. Was it possible? And now I knew he never cheated on me, I realized he was the one person who I had always been able to count on. Suddenly the answer was clear. "Okay."

"What?" My abrupt answer seemed to confuse him. He was ready to argue with me some more.

I exhaled, letting go of it all. Tate, Ralph, my images of him with another girl, my feelings of abandonment, all of which I'd been carrying with me for years. I put my hands on either side of his face. "I want to love you, Nash. I want to make this work. I've never stopped wanting. I only stopped hoping for it."

His eyes lightened, his brows unfurrowed, and he exhaled. He claimed my lips again, passion mingling with tears. And it all just dissolved, all the pain of the past. I knew I would still have some things to work out, but with Nash by my side, I suddenly felt I could do anything. He pulled away. "Will you stay with me tonight? I don't want you to be alone anymore."

I nodded, afraid if I spoke, the magic would somehow be broken.

"Good." He smiled broadly and gave me a kiss. "Welcome home, Chloe."

No words ever sounded finer.

We talked for a bit longer, about the future this time, and Nash's plans for the warehouse. Then, before we turned in, he decided to take another quick shower to wash away the blood and the grime from the alleyway, and hopefully relax his sore stomach muscles. While I waited, I meandered around his apartment. It wasn't very big, but I liked it. His bedroom contained a mattress and box springs on the floor, and a footstool with a lamp on it. The bed had a bright red comforter, which gave the room some cheer. The bathroom was in the hall, and pretty cramped, but the kitchen was a little roomier than one would expect, square, instead of rectangular, with a big fluorescent light to keep it bright, and some kind of viny plant, that looked abundantly healthy, on the window sill. There was probably room for a table for two by the one decent-sized window in the front room, but it looked like he used his couch and coffee table to dine on. He had a TV, set on a simple, wooden box with a hinged lid, and one end table with a lamp; that was all that would fit. The couch was white, as were the walls and carpeting, and I couldn't help but think of the whole place as a blank canvas. Along the wall farthest from the door, blocked canvases leaned in rows, three deep.

I squatted to look at them. They were exquisite. One held rows of purple flowers in a Tuscan field, with a house with the typical red roof and yellowed walls, and the comforting lines of poplars, straight and true, on either side of the house. It took my breath away. For some reason, I reached my hand out and touched it tenderly, as if to make sure it was real. The canvas next to it was a marvelous shot of the sky, at the moment when the sun sinks behind the clouds and turns their edges to a glowing, metallic sheen so beautiful it almost hurts to look at them. I noticed, in the corner, an easel with a canvas turned around on it. Curious, I stood and approached it. I glanced down the hall. Pale yellow light spilled out of the half-open door and I could hear Nash brushing his teeth. I knew I shouldn't snoop, but I was drawn to it. I peeked again in the direction of the bathroom, listening now to water running in the sink.

Tentatively, I reached out, and flipped the canvas around. I drew in a breath. The round "IMAGINE" mosaic from the park sprang to life, its pink and yellow flowered peace sign so convincing it was like I could smell its sweet scent.

So he did this today. In the short time he came home to change, he created this. I stepped forward, totally caught up in its beauty, peering more closely. I noticed he changed one thing about the mosaic. Instead of being made of hard, glossy marble, it was made of stone, crumbly around the edges, but still with that distinct quality of foreverness. It made the scene more living and breathing and warm, suiting the flowers, and the soft sunlight he captured angling down to illuminate the idea Lennon expressed in his song; imagine what the world would be like if we were all less selfish and more giving.

"What do you think?"

I jumped, turning to him, my face flushing. "I-I'm sorry. I shouldn't have been poking around."

"No. It's okay." He was toweling off his hair, and a few drops fell onto his bare chest, which I was trying my hardest not to ogle. Adulthood and a membership to the gym had given him the body of a young god. He jerked his head in the direction of the painting. "So, what do you think?"

I turned around and looked at it again, struck anew by its special magic. I couldn't speak for a moment. "It's...unbelievable."

He slid his arms around my waist. "I hoped you would like it." I leaned into him, feeling a contentment I hadn't known in ages.

"Are you tired?" he asked softly.

I nodded, but then giggled. "I guess I'm not used to that much biking. My thighs and calves are killing me."

"Maybe you should take a shower, too."

He brought me a T-shirt to change into, and left me alone. For the second time that day, I let the water caress my tired muscles, wondering about the change my life had taken. I smiled and hopped out of the shower, not wanting to be away from him any longer. When I walked into the bedroom, he was already in bed, sitting up with his back against the wall, reading something. He set his book aside and folded his arms behind his head, the light from the little footstool lamp helping to outline every muscle in his arms and chest. I froze.

"What are you doing?"

I shrugged, suddenly feeling awkward. What was the matter with me? This was my arena after all, my area of expertise. He sat, dropping his gorgeous arms easily in his lap. I had been with men built almost as nicely as he, close anyway, and while I admired them, aesthetically, I couldn't really say it was a huge turn-on. Sure, it helped to get me in the mood a little, but it didn't have the same heart-thumping, paralyzing effect as being with Nash did. What I did in the past was not for my pleasure, but for my sense of security, like a job. I took pride in being good at it, but I didn't enjoy it. Now I was scared shitless.

"Chloe? What's wrong? Are you having second thoughts about staying? You don't have to if you don't—"

"No."

He read my body language, and broke into a wide grin. "Come here. There's no reason to be nervous or uncomfortable around me. I want you to feel like this is your home as much as mine."

I gazed at him for another tick of the clock, and then a surge of happiness bubbled up inside of me like champagne from a fountain. I grinned and ran to him, diving onto the bed and into his arms. He laughed, rolling around with me, and squeezing me. Then we slowed, and quieted, still clutching each other securely, my eyes shut tight, breathing him in.

"I love you, Chloe Carmichael," he whispered in my ear, his voice strained. "I'm glad I have you back in my life."

"Me, too," I murmured, too overwhelmed to come up with more words to describe the way I felt when I was with him.

He rolled again, shifting his weight so he was beside me, looking down on me. "I can't believe it." He laughed. "Do you have any idea how many reality companies are in the phone book? And I picked yours?" He laughed again, a low, pleasant rumble.

"It's magic. You and I have always been magic," I returned simply. "Things just got...messed up."

"But not anymore. We've got a fresh start, and I'm going to make sure it works this time."

Tears sprang to my eyes. "I love you." I didn't think I would ever tire of saying that.

He kissed me. "And I love you."

He looked so handsome, his hair a little mussed from our goofing around, the lines of his face a little more chiseled than when we were in school together. In the lamplight, I brought my hands tentatively to his chest, appreciating every bench press which sculpted his muscles. I looked up, and I know he could see the desire swimming in my eyes.

He kissed me again, letting his hand slide down my leg, and then turning his head to follow his hand. "Your skin is *so* soft."

A shimmery feeling began in my stomach. At the same time, my face became hot.

He stroked the back of his hand down my face. "I love the way you blush."

I squirmed, ducking my head, feeling foolish. Sometimes it was difficult to have someone who could read you so easily. "Don't tease me."

He laughed softly, "I'm not."

He lifted my chin, and began to kiss me, his lips barely brushing mine, but his tongue teasing, leaving agonizing space between us until I arched and brought him more completely to me. His hand came to my hip, and for a split-second, a tinge of memory of the mugger's hand unnerved me, but I pushed it away. This was Nash, and his touch filled me with longing.

He ducked a finger under the edge of my string bikinis at my hip and trailed it back and forth for a few seconds before following the line of my panties downward. A shiver of pleasure ran through me and I bent my leg in response, sucking in my breath. He pulled his hand back, running it down my bent leg and back up, over my stomach, and up underneath the soft cotton T-shirt he gave me. His hand was cool against my skin, still warm from the shower, and strong, in control. He molded my breasts, one at a time, and moaned, shifting so more of his body was on top of mine. Moving his hand down to the back of my thigh on my bent leg, he squeezed me. My hand slipped around his waist and I clutched his back, wanting to feel his weight on me, wanting all of him. As if in response, he let his leg come all the way over, straddling me, pelvis-to-pelvis. Our kisses became more urgent, almost frantic. Then, without warning, he straightened his arms, pulling himself away from me, but staring down into my face. He was breathing hard and his eyes held a look of wild confusion, as if he was trying to remember why he stopped.

"Chloe, I know this sounds crazy—I guess I'm horribly old-fashioned—but I still want to wait to make love to you until our wedding night. What do you think about that? Are you okay with it?"

At the current moment, not so much. But I guess I'll get used to it.

I nodded, trying to calm my raging heart and hormones. But then, when I looked into his eyes, so loving and kind, I wanted so much to show him how much I cared for him. I was so grateful for a second chance, and I wanted to please him so much.

"Lay down," I said quietly.

"Huh?"

"Lay down," I repeated, and he flopped on his pillow. I rose up on my elbow, mimicking his former position. I started kissing his chest, working my way down, my hands on his sides. But when he realized what I was intending to do, he reached down and grabbed my shoulders to stop me.

"No. No!" he practically shouted, his voice showing a hint of panic. I stopped my movements. "I don't want you to do that."

I sat and hugged my knees to my chest, flashing back to a million other times when I felt cheap and dirty. But I never thought Nash would make me feel that way.

He sat quickly. "Oh, no, Chloe. I'm sorry. I didn't mean to hurt your feelings."

I turned away from him, my heart burning in my chest from mortification and my throat almost unbearably tight. This is what I knew would happen. He would see me for who I really was and it would sicken him. Everything inside of me seemed to cyclone out of control. With a *whoosh* my shame hit me and sucked me into a shaking blackness. He touched my arm, and I recoiled, not wanting to mar him, not wanting this one good thing in my life ruined by what I had become. Tears rose in my eyes, and I wished, somehow, I could hide myself from him.

"Chloe, honey, please." His voice begged me, and I realized already some of my pain was his.

"It's okay," I said, my voice shaky. "I understand." *I understand I'm nothing but a whore and you don't want me.* "Umm. I'm going to go now. I forgot, I have an early meeting in the morning." I scrambled out of bed, grabbed my neat little stack of clothes and got into the bathroom to change before he could do anything.

He knocked and called my name, but I didn't answer. As I pulled my dress on over my head, I caught my face in the mirror. I was pale and drawn, my eyes hollow, and I almost broke down then. But I told myself I needed to get it together enough to get home, then I'd have my meltdown. When I opened the door, I caught him in mid-pace.

"Please don't go."

"I have to. It's okay. I'll be okay," I assured him and myself at the same time. I blew past him without looking in his eyes.

"Clo..." He made an exasperated sound in his throat. "Well, if you're leaving, at least let me take you home. I'll walk up and get my truck and be back in five minutes." He headed for the bedroom to get some pants.

"No. That's okay. I already called a cab," I lied. "I need to go. He's waiting for me."

I heard his protests as I closed the door behind me, but I kept going. On the way down, my heels kept sliding through the openings in his fire escape threatening to catapult me off into space, so I slipped them off, flying down the stairs as fast as I could. When I got to the street, he opened his door and came charging down the steps, calling my name. For once, luck was with me, and a cabbie was taking a nap right outside his building. We sped away and hit the first light as Nash emerged on the sidewalk in front.

CHAPTER FIFTEEN

Nash

I stood in my bedroom doorway looking at the rumpled sheets where she had lain a few moments before, my head still spinning. I felt like I swallowed a lead ball. Like every breath was short of meeting my needs. She wouldn't even look at me. I knew all she wanted to do was please me, and I made her feel like crap, right when we started to work things out. I should have known better than to ask her to stay over. She was so vulnerable right now. She had laid her whole, dark life open to me, which was incredibly brave, but it also made her fragile. And then when she...wow. The things she did to me. I didn't know what to do.

As angry as I was at myself, the longer I sat thinking about it, I still couldn't figure out any other way I could have handled things better, except for coming up with words to explain myself afterward. But, to be honest, I am amazed I was able to speak at all. Being with her like that, together, in my bed...it completely demolished my capacity for rational thought. She had a way of touching me that absolutely annihilated all thought at all; I became a feeling, reacting organism swimming in pleasing sensations and craving more.

With a groan, I fell stiffly on my bed, face first. I was looking at valuable merchandise through a glass case. I knew what I wanted, and it was so beautiful and shiny, but I couldn't get at it. Something always kept getting in our way. Usually me.

That didn't mean I would give up trying. I grabbed my phone receiver from off the floor, where I carelessly set it at some point, and then realized I didn't even know her number. I trudged into the kitchen, my sore muscles beginning to complain, and rifled through my "everything drawer" until I found my copy of the phone book, minus its cover.

I got the damn voice mail. "Chloe...this is Nash." I sighed. I should have thought out what I was going to say before I called. "You left before I had a chance to explain myself—arr! I hate leaving messages..." I sighed again, frustrated with my struggle to find the right words. "I love you, Clo. I didn't mean to hurt you. I would never mean to... The thing is, babe...when I make love to you for the first time, on our wedding night, I want to be able to see your pretty face. Ugh! I'm not saying this right. I want it to mean something. I want it to be special." I paused so long I was afraid the machine may have clicked off, but I started again anyway. "I don't know why it's so important to me. Any man would have been a fool to refuse you tonight. Please just call me so I can talk to you." I ended in disgust.

Five minutes later I called back.

"Okay. Maybe you don't feel like talking tonight. I can understand that. But could you call so I know you made it home okay? I need to know you're all right."

Fifteen minutes later, I called back again. I got a busy signal. At least I knew she was home. Fifteen minutes after that, I got a busy signal again and after trying a few more times, finally came to the conclusion she took her phone off the hook. I thought about the way she looked when she opened the door when I came and picked her up before dinner—gorgeous and sexy, and so hopeful. I thought about her across the table from me, her eyes bright in the candlelight. I thought about her in my bed.

And I took a cold shower.

When I turned the water off, the phone was ringing. "Shit!" I grabbed a towel, but ran dripping, from the bathroom in time to hear it stop ringing. I waited then pushed the button for voicemail. Her voice sounded tired and stuffy, no doubt because she had been crying.

"I'm home, Nash, and I'm...fine." She didn't sound convincing. "I guess we were foolish to hope..." Her voice drifted off. After a long pause she spoke again, her voice strained. "I love you, too. I guess I'll always love you. But I suppose it's true what they say, you can't go home again. ...I think we both realized tonight I'm not the same girl I used to be. And I'm certainly not the blushing bride you want. You shouldn't apologize for wanting that. You deserve it. And being that way is what makes you Nash. I would never want to change you." Another long pause. "I hope you find what you want, Nash. I really do. I guess I wished I could be that for you, but—let's face it—I'm not. I'm just not. Please don't come by to see me, it confuses things. You need to know, though, I don't regret one minute of my time with you. Every second was precious. Goodbye."

I listened dully to the *beep* as the machine shut off. Once again I did nothing but make her completely miserable. And myself, to boot. Maybe she was right. Maybe I should let her go. Maybe we made such a muddle of things we could never put it behind us. I would have to leave her alone, give her time to heal on her own. And never go back to her.

But, as much as I meant it, I couldn't do it. The next morning, I called her office to put a bid on the warehouse.

Chloe

It had been two weeks since I saw or heard from Nash. Today was his closing on the warehouse. It was circled in red on my calendar. Big, red, concentric circles. Jack was in a hellacious mood as I hadn't given in to his demands to crawl under his desk and do him while his secretary took dictation. I hadn't been with anyone. It was an all-time record for me. But I no longer looked at my little trysts as a way to have power over men. I saw them plainly for what they were, a pathetic attempt to establish some sort of control over my life. I didn't want it anymore. Having seen myself through Nash's eyes, I was sick to my stomach whenever I thought about who I had become.

And Jack was royally pissed about it.

I could hear him now, blustering at my secretary who had enough problems handling Nash's persistent phone calls for me. I mean, there were only so many meetings one could be in during the course of a day, right? She had become pretty inventive though, even telling him once I was down in Payroll handling a paycheck dispute. But now she barely got to her feet, with a feeble, "I think Ms. Carmichael is with a client—" when Jack blew past her, yanking the door of my office open.

"Jack," I said coolly, drumming my fingernails on the top edge of a file folder I'd just closed.

"*Ms.* Carmichael," he returned with an edge. "I expect you're ready for the Nabry closing?"

The mention of his name made me wince, but I recovered quickly. "Of course."

"Then let's get this over with. No sense putting it off."

He stormed back out of my office, expecting me to follow. I glanced at my watch. It was 9:30; our meeting was at 10:30 downtown, about a half-hour away. We'd be way early. Still, I wanted the whole thing over with, too. I jumped up and followed him. I had no idea why he insisted on joining me for the closing, which I would normally handle myself, with one of our lawyers in tow, but Jack "wanted to be sure this Nabry fellow didn't try to take advantage of me."

I'd thought about a million times about calling Jack and turning the whole thing over to him. But part of me said that was taking the easy way out, and that was rarely good. Maybe this closing would be what it was billed to be, a closing, once and for all, of that chapter of my life. But, as much as I hated admitting it to myself, part of me was also anxious to see Nash, one more time. How pathetic was that? I gave masochism a whole new name.

I hurried to keep up with Jack's long strides. On the ride over, he kept sliding his hand between my legs, and I inched closer to the door, which seemed to infuriate him all the more. Why couldn't he get the hint? I decided that part of my life was over. I'd go it alone. I was making enough money now to support myself, and the high I got from getting men off was gone. I'll admit, it made for lonely nights. Nights of staring at the shadows on my ceiling, wondering where my life would take me.

But there was no time to think of that now. We were stuck in a snarl of traffic and I had to ward off Mr. Handsy. By the time we got to Nash's attorney's high-rise office building, I had a red mark on my upper thigh from where Jack finally decided to latch on. As soon as he pulled into a parking spot, I prepared to jump out of the vehicle. He turned as I got out.

"Chloe, come back here for a minute," he said, his motives transparent. I knew exactly what he wanted from me in that parking garage and he was going to be disappointed.

"No, Jack. Come on. We're late." I strode brusquely across the concrete floor of the garage, my heels ringing. I would never take a ride to a meeting from Jack Duran again, not that he gave me much of a choice this morning. He got out and hurried after me, practically growling.

He didn't say anything on the ride up in the glass elevator. It was located in the center of the atrium, beyond a huge fountain, which, I think, had goldfish in it. As we approached the glass-fronted office I could see Nash look up and take notice of me. He rose out of his chair, causing his three-piece lawyer, David Suchmore, to swivel in his chair, his mouth still forming a sentence. Nash looked good. He looked *really* good. He had on an expensive-looking dress shirt which was a smoky blue color, and slate-grey pants. My pulse went up, and my eyes went down. How would I get through this meeting?

Nash and David were standing when we entered. Our lawyer, Lambert Godfrey, remained seated, smiling comfortably at us.

"Jack," David said, shaking my boss's hand. "Ms. Carmichael." David gave me a glowing smile, which I ignored. He had been one of my conquests. We shook hands.

"Mr. Nabry," Jack said coldly, offering his hand. Nash nodded curtly. Jack always called him by his first name up until now. I wasn't sure what the hostility was about, but I didn't really care much either. I wanted to get this over with and get out of here. I offered Nash my hand, uncomfortably.

"Nash." My voice came out choked, and I cleared my throat to hide my awkwardness. He held my hand a heartbeat longer than necessary, and I looked up into his warm brown eyes and found myself lost for a second. Jack tugged on my suit sleeve, and I hastily sat next to him, across the table from Nash and Lambert.

"Jack." Lambert shook hands. "Chloe, how are you?"

I found my voice. "Fine, Lambert. Thanks for asking." He was a good guy. One of the few "happily married" men at the office who hadn't made a pass at me. "I heard you and your wife had another boy. Congratulations."

"Thanks. Yeah, he's a little cutie. I'll bring him by your office next week."

I smiled genuinely. "That would be nice."

"If Chloe, here, is done with the chit-chatting...?" Jack sneered.

"Certainly," I responded, surprised by his tone.

Jack got down to business, but Nash seemed to be having trouble following. He kept peering at me, and I looked anywhere else. Finally, Jack snapped, "Chloe, why don't you make yourself useful and fetch us all some coffee. Black, two sugars."

I sat stunned for a moment. It had been years—since I was a junior exec, in fact—since I was relegated to coffee duty.

"Well," he said impatiently, "the coffee doesn't have legs." He made walking motions in the air with two fingers. "Get going, Chloe. I'm sure you'll have no problem getting Mr. Nabry, here, whatever he wants."

My face colored; his implication was clear. I thought about several things I wanted to say to Jack, each of which would get me fired on the spot. Instead, I pushed back my chair and stood, turning to Nash. "Nash?" I said uncertainly, fighting back tears of humiliation.

"No, Chloe. I don't want anything," Nash said quickly, appalled. "And if I did, I'd be perfectly capable of getting some myself. As is everyone in this room," he added pointedly, staring at Jack, who paged through papers, ignoring him.

"Lambert?"

The young lawyer seemed equally shocked. "No, that's all right, Chloe. I've already got tea," he answered, smiling at me.

I nodded, bolstered by his kindness. "David?"

"Cream and sugar," David answered without looking up. I hastened out of the office, asking the secretary outside where I could get some coffee. When I got back, Jack and Nash were in a heated debate about some minor detail.

"That price did not include the parking lot," Jack was saying.

"How can I run a business without a parking lot?" Nash barked back.

"Well, excuse me for saying so, Mr. Nabry, but I'm sure you'll have more than enough parking for the hordes of people who will be flocking to your little art gallery." Jack knew damn well the parking lot was considered part of the property.

Nash was halfway out of his seat when I interrupted. "I'm afraid I may have given Nash the impression that the parking lot was included with the price."

"Well, dammit, Chloe, you should have checked your specs."

I set Jack's coffee in front of him carefully. "I'm sure," I said through gritted teeth, "we can find a way to work this into the agreement. After all," I said, looking Jack in the eyes, "this piece of property has been on the books for a while, and getting rid of it would be a plus."

"Well, that doesn't mean I'm giving it away," Jack sniped, but he finally conceded. "Okay, I guess we can throw that in."

As I set down David's coffee, I caught him trying to look down my blouse. I put my hand to my chest to close the gap. He leered at me, making my skin crawl.

By the time we were finished, I was dreaming of a vodka gimlet and a couple of Tylenol. Jack gathered the final copies together and handed it to me to put in a filer. As I tapped them to straighten them, Jack knocked my hand, sending the papers to the floor.

"Geez, Chloe. Can't you even keep the paperwork in order?" he complained as I turned to scoop them off the floor.

"You freakin' knocked her hand!" Nash screamed, jumping to his feet in a rage.

"You know, *Nash,* now that I have your signature on the dotted line, I don't have to be nice to you anymore."

"Nor do I." Nash took a swing at Jack, catching him squarely in the jaw. Jack, who had just stood, flew back into his chair, which rolled, hitting the glass wall of the office with a loud crash. People in outer offices gawked as David stepped in to hustle Nash out of the office. He looked up at me apologetically as David pushed him through the door and toward the elevator. I stood, dumbfounded, my gaze returning to Jack, who was turning three shades of purple.

"Why that son-of-a-bitch." He got up and charged toward the door, but I slowed him down by getting in front of him and pushing him back by the shoulders.

"Dammit, Chloe. Get out of the way or, so help me God, I will send you through this glass."

"Jack!" Lambert roared, surprising us both. He was a fairly mild-mannered man. "If you so much as lay a hand on her I'll testify in court you have been a complete and total ass today toward her. And Mr. Nabry beat me to the punch, literally." His words hung in the air between the three of us like a huge bubble.

"My own people..." Jack grumbled. He turned and headed out the door.

I sighed. "Thank you, Lambert." I hastily straightened out the papers.

"Anytime, Chloe," he returned grimly, still staring at Jack's back through the glass wall. I could tell he was proud of himself, though, for standing up to the giant of a man who used to play football for Augustana.

I gave him a smile, jammed the papers into my folder, and scrambled after Jack. I ducked into the elevator as it was about to close. It was just me and Jack. I breathed heavily from my little dash, and that was the only sound for a while. Jack reached out and slammed the emergency button. The elevator jerked to a stop between floors and I had to reach back and grab the handrail to keep from being thrown to the floor. He turned on me, his enormous frame towering over me like some ogre.

"You know what, Chloe. I was fine with sharing you with Taylor McNulty, and Sam Rider, and the other guys."

I drew in a breath. What? Did they have some sort of network? Had they all compared notes on how Ms. Chloe Carmichael was in the sack?

"But this guy. This guy's a...an outsider," he blustered. "And, as if it's not bad enough my wife won't put out, now you, all of a sudden—Chloe Carmichael, of all people—have become a coldhearted bitch. Well, I won't have it. Either you give it to me hot and hard right now, or you walk." He pushed me up against the elevator and began grabbing me. Everything inside of me screamed. I put my hands on his shoulders and pushed, squirming and shouting at him. His shock and surprise worked to my advantage as he was slow to react and I got him off-balance. I got him far enough away from me I could start shoving him, hitting him as hard as I could in the shoulders and backing him up, my hands turning to fists, pounding him relentlessly as I shrieked at him.

"Get your filthy hands off me, Jack Duran. You don't own me and you can't tell me how to live my life. That old Chloe is dead. Dead. Do you hear? And so help me, if you try to fire me I'll come at you with both barrels and with Lambert Godfrey by my side and we will take you down. You... got... it?" I punctuated each word with a hard poke to the chest.

"Yeah, Chloe," he responded quietly. "I've got it."

"Good." I turned on my heel and punched at the emergency button. The elevator sprang to life and I stood with my arms crossed, still shaking with fury. When it came to a stop, I yelled back over my shoulder. "I'm taking a cab and charging it to your account."

CHAPTER SIXTEEN

Nash

I couldn't stand that prick Jack Duran. The way he treated Chloe. And she sat there and took it. I wanted more than one shot at him. But David, who I could now see was his asshole friend, shooed me out, rambling on about assault charges and jail time the whole way down in the elevator. When we got to the lobby, I charged out of the elevator and began pacing back and forth while David continued to lecture me about my behavior until I reminded him his money came from me and he better shut the hell up, which he did and walked away.

With a sigh I flopped on a couch in a conversation area whose chat-friendly design was lost on me, at the moment. A loud, grinding noise had me raising my gaze to the glass elevator, which had come to an abrupt stop between floors. When I saw Chloe inside, I jumped to my feet in alarm. I watched that big, burly prince of a boss of hers push her up against the wall, his big fat hands grabbing her chest. I moved forward, although, what I could do in my position was beyond me, my capability for flight somewhat hindered by the whole gravity thing. I watched as Chloe backed him off, shoving him and advancing on him until she had him in a corner, all five-foot-plus of her. I could tell she was screaming at him furiously, and whatever she was saying must have packed a wallop, too, as Duran began to hang his head. Finally, she turned her back on him and stood rigidly in the elevator until the doors opened up. I ran across the lobby to intercept her.

"Chloe, can I talk to you?"

"Nash." Her expression was pained. "There's nothing left to say."

"Please, Chloe. I need to explain."

Jack strode up behind her, putting his big meaty hands on her shoulders. "Is this guy bothering you?"

She turned her head to glare at him and he gingerly removed his hands. "I think we both know I can take care of myself, Jack," she said meaningfully.

"Well...I don't like you talking to this guy." He pouted. "I don't trust him. And... you're not going anywhere with him," he ended, trying to regain some footing.

"If I want to go with Nash—"

"You do, and you won't work for me—or any other realtor in this city—again."

Her jaw dropped, and then her voice turned icy. "You do that, Jack. You fire me. And Lambert Godfrey will have me sitting behind your desk in a year's time. You think about that. Come on, Nash." She stuck her arm stubbornly through mine and we walked off. "Where is your car?" she asked out of the side of her mouth, trying to be inconspicuous as she glanced back to see if Jack was following us. But the brute was stopped in his tracks by her words.

We marched out, through the revolving glass doors, and into the bright sunlight.

To my surprise, she threw her head back and laughed when we reached the other side. "Ha. Ha." She threw her arms out from her sides as if embracing the sunshine. "That felt good. That felt *really* good."

I smiled at her. "You were fantastic."

She stared at me as if seeing me for the first time and her wonderful smile faded. She stood transfixed for several seconds before saying quietly, "I'm sorry. But this is over." She turned to walk away from me.

She got several feet before I yelled, "But I love you, Chloe!" Several people stared at me after my outburst—some smiling, some frowning—but I had eyes only for Chloe. She turned and gave me an appraising look, then walked slowly back to me.

"We need to go someplace private."

"I know just the place." I jangled my new keys in front of her.

"We need to get something to drink first."

We went to the store and picked up a bottle of wine. I half expected her to be gone when I got back to the truck, but she was good for her word. We didn't talk much on the way over. I think we were both strategizing, with different ends in mind. She wanted to convince me I was better off without her; I wanted to convince her without her there was nothing.

I was happy to see her brighten a little bit as we pulled into the parking lot of my new warehouse. Something was magical for her about this warehouse;

that was easy to see. The magic it held for me was in her eyes. She waited impatiently for me to mess with the lock, and then bolted in when I pulled the big door back. When I came in, she was standing as she was the first time, in the golden shafts of light from the skylights, looking up with a faraway look in her eyes.

"This is going to be such a great gallery and studio for you. The light is perfect, and visitors won't feel confined as they look at your pictures. So they can totally immerse themselves in them...and meander..." As she spoke, she strolled carelessly through imagined rows of artwork, her hands folded behind her back. I needed her so badly. Her enthusiasm, her perspective, her appreciation for my paintings...

"Can I invite you up to my bedroom?" I asked abruptly.

She stopped in her tracks, unsure of how to respond, but her good feelings carried over into her response. "Are you trying to seduce me, Mr. Nabry?" she asked with a hint of a smile.

"Possibly, Ms. Carmichael." I grabbed her hand and ran across the warehouse, racing up the steps, laughing. I pulled her through the doorway into the room which would be my bedroom. I sat on the floor, and motioned for her to sit, too, while I wrestled the cork out of the bottle. But, instead, she went to look out of a small, square window on the back wall. When I came to her with the glass of wine, she jumped, startled from her thoughts, and knocked my hands, spilling a little onto the hardwood floor, and some down my front.

"Oh, Nash. I'm so sorry." She took the glasses from me and put them on the floor. I brushed at my wet pants and then straightened. She noticed a spot near my collar and brushed there.

"It's okay. It's f-ine." My voice broke. She was so close I could hear her heartbeat. She gazed up into my eyes, and I stepped forward boldly and our lips met. Her fingers went immediately to my hair as she pulled me in, our mouths meeting again and again, in a fevered rush. I pressed her against the wall to the right of the window, rubbing her sides with my hands roughly. Suddenly, the image of Jack Duran pressing against her in the elevator flashed through my mind, and I stepped back.

Desire faded in her eyes, replaced with confusion. I walked away from her, my hands on my hips. "I'm sorry. I don't want you to think I was using you the way those other men did."

"I know you're not that way," she said softly.

I turned to face her, surprised.

"I've had a lot of time to think about things lately...and I understand now you have been the *only* one, or one of the few anyway, who has always been honest with me and cared for me." She gazed unflinchingly into my eyes and stepped forward. My entire body went on alert. When she was within a foot of me, she reached up and tenderly touched my face. "I want to thank you, for all you've been to me. My friend, at first," she swallowed, seeming to steel herself to continue, "and always so much more than that." She glanced down at my lips briefly and passed her thumb over them, then looked me again in the eye, taking a shuddering breath. "I will *always* love you, Nash Nabry," she said slowly, emphasizing each word. "And I hope...I hope you'll find the person you're looking for, because you deserve that." I started to speak, but she put a finger over my lips, closing her eyes for a moment. "*Please*, let me finish." I stilled, so enchanted by her. "I'm sorry. I'm sorry for having ruined everything between us, for throwing it all away. I really am, and I wanted you to know that." She turned to walk away, but I grabbed her elbow and spun her around.

"You can't take all the blame for what happened between us. I had a piece in that, too. I may not have cheated on you, but, for a brief period of time, I put my studies before you, and that was wrong. Maybe if I tried harder to reach you, you wouldn't have believed Tate when he lied to you. And as far as the person I'm looking for, she's right here with me now."

She shook her head. "No. I'm not that person. I—"

I was suddenly angry with her. She was so stubborn. How could I get it through her thick head that I loved her? I decided to use my anger. "So, what? Now you're the judge, jury and executioner of our relationship?" I barked.

She was taken aback. "Wh-what?"

"Since when do you get to decide what is right for me?" She opened her mouth to interrupt, but I talked over her. "You've done all the talking. Now it's my turn," I shouted, my voice ricocheting off the walls in the empty warehouse. She blinked, but shut her mouth. I softened a little. "You told me about all you've been through—which was very brave of you, by the way. You laid it out for me, without trying to hide anything," I thought about this. "Do you understand how astonishing that is? Anyway, you told me these things, but now *I* get to decide what I want to do about them." I paused, and she watched me carefully. "You tell me these things have changed you, and I'm sure they have...but..." I struggled with the words, wanting to get them right. "I understand now not only what you did, but I also understand *why* you did it, and that part of you hasn't changed, the part of you that is good, and pure and wholesome—"

"How can you say that?" she protested. "Look at what I've *done*."

"Those are just acts, Chloe. It's why you chose them, that is important. You chose them because you were hurt by me, so I have to shoulder some of the blame for that. You chose them because you had to survive, and no one can blame you for that. And you chose them because you needed to feel like someone loved you. We all need that. And everyone you loved failed you—your dad—through no fault of his own, but because someone *took* his life from him—your mom—who was sick, but who still owed you her protection—and me. Not because I cheated, but because I failed to be there for you, physically and emotionally." The tears trickled down her face as I continued. I decided to take a gamble. I was pretty sure I understood Chloe, but it still was a chance. "Why did you push Jack away in the elevator?"

She seemed confused by the change of subjects. "Why did I...?"

I nodded. "Why did you push him away when he was grabbing you?"

"Because...because...I didn't want him to touch me that way."

"Why? A month ago, if I understand you right, you not only wouldn't have had a problem with him grabbing you, you would have encouraged it, right?" Her face turned red, and I knew my gamble would pay off. "So why did you not want him to touch you that way today? Was it because you were mad at him, because he was treating you like dirt in the conference room?"

"Well, yes, sort of."

"But there was more to it than that, wasn't there?"

"Yes," she blustered, her own ire rising. "Yes. I didn't want him touching me like that anymore. I didn't want anyone touching me like that anymore."

"Why?"

"Because, since I talked to you...it's not the same. I don't want that."

"What don't you want?" I pressed. I could see how enraged and upset she was becoming and part of me wanted to sweep her up in my arms and comfort her, but part of me understood I needed to push her further. She was silent, and it was as if I could see her mind searching for an answer to my question. "What don't you want anymore, Chloe?" I said coolly.

"It doesn't give me the same feeling of control, of power. It's pathetic. It leaves me empty, or worse, makes me feel dirty and bad. I don't want to feel that way."

"And why did that change?" I asked softly, coming closer to her.

"Because of you," she whispered. "Because I couldn't stand for you to think of me...that way."

I stepped up now; I couldn't bear not comforting her. I brushed away the tears from her face. "I don't think of you that way. The fact you don't want that kind of life anymore shows me you haven't changed inside from when I knew you. It was all an act, a way of fooling yourself into feeling okay about yourself, into feeling worthwhile." I paused, my hands around her arms. "You told me what happened to you after you left, but I never explained what happened to me after that night. When you weren't there to answer my calls, I came back to look for you. Word around town was you'd moved away. My whole world was shattered. But...I think part of me never gave up hope of finding you again. I haven't been with another woman, not even thought twice about it, for all this time." I put my hands on either side of her face. "Chloe, I love you—uncontrollably, unalterably—I love you. Do you still love me?"

"You know I do," she answered without hesitation.

I kissed her, once. "Do you want me to be happy?" I asked, searching her eyes.

"Yes," she breathed with vehemence.

"The only way I will be happy is if I'm by your side from here on out. Can you do that?"

She closed her eyes and a single tear slid out. I held my breath, knowing what happened next could be my undoing. But, to my astonishment, she nodded her head jerkily. I kissed her, and then held her, in silence, while the minutes ticked away.

"I love you," I whispered.

"I know."

After a time, a thought dawned on me, and I chuckled and pulled back. "Why do you like this place so much?"

She looked at me, a smile slowly spreading across her face. "Do you know why?"

"I have my suspicions."

She looked around at the wooden beamed rafters. Smaller skylights were cut up here, but still, plenty of light. It was an unusual warehouse, more like a large barn, I guess. "It reminds me of the clubhouse," she murmured finally.

I laughed. "That's what I thought." I left her and brought the wine glasses back. "Can we have our toast now?"

She nodded brightly.

"To this place, to us, and to new beginnings."

CHAPTER SEVENTEEN

Chloe

Nash and I had been working hard on cleaning up the warehouse for months, and we made quite a bit of progress on the bottom floor. It was in surprisingly good shape, repair-wise, but it was filthy. We decided to tear down the wall upstairs ourselves, after having an architect friend of mine guarantee me it wasn't a load-bearing wall.

So, one day, near the end of summer, with a flourish, Nash handed me the wrecking-hammer and allowed me first swing. Then we went at it together until all that was left was rubble and two sweaty workers, covered in drywall dust.

Nash laughed.

"What?" I wiped a bead of sweat from my brow. He set down his hammer and came over to kiss me, which we had been doing a lot of, after having finally sorted out all of our past problems. This tended to slow down the work some, but we didn't mind. In fact, I was thinking now I liked the fact he chose to take his T-shirt off today, although I was almost certain he caught me fantasizing about him a couple of times.

"You look so cute with your bandana on, all smiley, covered in dust."

I laughed. "Yeah, right."

He slid his hands to my hips and rocked me back and forth and chuckled again, wiping some dust from my cheek. "You really are a mess. You look like you've been dunked in flour. Ooh. Interesting image..."

I swatted him playfully. "Stop."

"Okay. Why don't we call it a day and grab showers?"

"Sounds fantastic."

"And then you'll be wanting to get dressed up for tonight," he mumbled as he bent to scoop his T-shirt up from the floor.

"For tonight?" I asked suspiciously, a smile playing on my lips. "Why's that?"

He shrugged. "We might be celebrating." When he bent to gather up the tools, I ran and jumped on his back.

"Don't tease me." I giggled. "You know I hate it when you do that."

He straightened, grabbing my legs so I was riding piggyback. "No you don't," he countered, turning his head so he could kiss the arm wrapped around his shoulder.

"You're right. I love it. But spill it, boy. I wanna know what's up."

"All right." He swung me around and set me on the ground to face him. "I sold a painting," he said matter-of-factly.

"You what?" I whooped. "Which one?"

"The Imagine one."

"Oh." Why did it have to be that one? I loved that one. I tried to recover my enthusiasm. "Congratulations."

He frowned. "You don't seem all that thrilled."

"No. I mean, yes. I am. It's just...I *really* liked that one."

"But you're only pretending to like the other ones?"

"No." I swatted his arm again. "You know what I mean. It was special...because—"

"Because of our day in the park."

"Yes."

"Well, I don't think you'll mind much when you see it hanging. Come on."

He grabbed my hand and led me outside, but I sighed, unable to curb my disappointment.

When he showed up at my place a few hours later, he whistled in appreciation as he held his hand up so I could spin under it. He had given me enough time to grab a new dress. It was red and was tight around the curves, with like a quarter inch of sheer black material at the top of the bodice which wrapped straight around me. The bottom hem was pleated, giving it a slightly mermaidy effect, and it was short, showing off my new black heels. "Wow, babe. You've outdone yourself." I had put my hair up into a sleek knot, off to one side, allowing curls to spill down one shoulder. Coincidentally, he wore a red dress shirt and black pants.

"Man. It looks like we color-coordinated. So where are we going?" I nagged, unable to curb my curiosity.

"All you need to know is—we can walk from here."

"You're joking." I frowned. There weren't any restaurants near here, were there?

We walked up the street, then cut over and crossed into Central Park West. "We're not going to walk back this way, are we? I'm not sure about the park after dark."

"I've got us a ride home," he responded with a sly smile.

"Do ya now?" I grinned. "You know this whole mysterious-guy thing is really working for me."

"I thought it might," he returned smugly.

We walked along the sidewalk outside of Tavern on the Green. Outdoor lights were strung in the trees around one section of the restaurant and it looked like someone sprinkled fairy dust on it. "It's so beautiful, isn't it?"

"Yes, it is." Nash turned and headed up the sidewalk toward the building.

"Oh, do you think we should check it out while people are eating?"

"No, silly. We're eating here."

"Oh, honey," I said, afraid to disappoint him. "You have to have reservations here, months in advance—"

"Unless you recently sold the owner a painting."

"Here?" I screeched, drawing some attention from nearby diners, but I didn't care. "It's hanging here? You're joking me."

"No," he said, laughing. "It's hanging here."

"You are joking!" I screamed again, incredulous. He ushered me into an entrance and there it was, hanging prominently above an inner doorway. "Oh." My heart stopped. There it was. Our painting, hanging at Tavern on the Green in Central Park. "Oh, my gosh," I breathed.

He laughed. "You're not supposed to cry."

"Am I crying?" I patted my cheeks and found them wet. "It's just...it's like a dream come true to see your artwork displayed where so many people can enjoy it."

"I know," he said, squeezing my hand. "Are you okay with my selling it now?"

"Of course. This is where it belongs."

"Good. We still have a little time before our reservations. Do you want to take a quick walk while it's still light outside?"

"Sure, that would be nice."

We strolled through the trees, with his arm around my shoulder. It was a gorgeous night. A soft wind rustled the tree branches and I mused over what a wonderful turn my life had taken. The past several weeks with Nash had been incredible. I felt like I reclaimed a part of myself long lost. Strangely, even things with Jack were better. I earned his begrudging respect as I topped all sellers in the month of June. I found out, when I wasn't too busy trying to bed every other realtor on the planet, I was pretty good at selling property. And working with Nash on the warehouse, having a joint project like that, was really fun, and rewarding. In a month or two, he would be open for business. And what a dynamite start this was, to have his painting hanging where thousands of potential buyers could see it.

Nash stopped walking and I looked around. We had come to the very spot he captured in his painting, the Imagine mosaic. I sighed happily. He took his arm from around my shoulder and took both of my hands in his.

"You know, you asked me when we first came here what I was thinking about, and I didn't tell you. But I'd like to tell you now."

I nodded solemnly. He suddenly seemed so serious. Did I really want to know what he had been thinking?

"I was 'imagining' a life with you. A life where we could hold hands," he looked down at our hands, "and walk together in Central Park. A life where we could build a future, like what we're doing at the warehouse. A life together, you and I, husband and wife, where we could raise children and change the world simply by loving each other. Now," he said hesitantly, digging in his pocket for something. "I know this is quick..." to my astonishment he pulled out a ring box and knelt down, right at the base of the mosaic. "But I have loved you all of my life, and I would be so honored if you would consider taking my name and becoming my wife. You don't have to answer now—"

"No. No. No," I shouted, jumping up and down.

He paled. "Well, wait now. Think about it before you turn me down."

"No. I mean yes. I don't have to think about it, Nash. I love you." I yanked him to his feet and grabbed his face and kissed him, saying more quietly, "I love you."

By this time, we were both crying, after everything we went through, it was almost too good to be true. "Can I show you the ring?"

I nodded.

He opened the little black box still in his hand. I gasped. I was so unbearably happy I had to lighten the moment a little. "Man. How much did you make that poor man pay for your painting? I'm kidding," I added quickly. "Oh. It's so beautiful." He slipped it on my finger and it fit like a glove. He sighed.

"I can't believe how well it fits. You don't have any rings I could judge it against, so I left the sizing for later. But I don't think we'll have to do anything to it." He squeezed me around the middle. Eventually we strolled back in the direction from which we'd come. I kept gazing at the ring on my finger and screaming inside, *I'm marrying Nash!*

"Oh, and I didn't buy it," he interjected, motioning to the ring. "It was my mom's." My mouth dropped open. "She wanted you to have it," he reassured me. "She insisted, in fact, last time we went to visit her."

Weeks ago, we'd made the trip home to visit Nash's mom and brothers. I was nervous. He had told me his mom was much better than when I last saw her, but I was still afraid she wouldn't recognize me. She was much more like a mom to me than my own mom, in the end, and I knew it would hurt if she didn't know who I was.

When we got there, I was surprised by how much she had aged in the few short years since I'd seen her. She was in a wheelchair; a second stroke had robbed her of some of her motor skills. But when we walked in, her eyes sparkled and she reached for my hand.

"Well, hello," she said warmly.

Tears sprang to my eyes. She did remember. I bent so I was on eye level with her. "Oh, I was afraid it had been so long you wouldn't recognize me."

"Of course I recognize you. You're Nash's wife." My heart plummeted, and I looked up at Nash, crushed, at a loss for what to say to her. But she continued, "Chloe." She patted my hand softly. "Of course I remember my Nash's Chloe."

"Oh." I was so overwhelmed by emotion I couldn't continue the conversation. Luckily Nash bailed me out.

"Chloe's been in the car a long time, Mom. She probably needs to clean up. Do you know where the restroom is?" he asked me.

I nodded gratefully, finding my voice at last. "I saw it when I came in. I'll be right back, Mrs. Nabry."

"Now, you call me Evie, or Mom. You're getting too old for this Mrs. Nabry stuff."

I nodded and fled to the bathroom to compose myself.

I looked back warmly on that day now. "She gave the ring to you while we were there?"

He laughed. "No. First she scolded me for not having married you yet, and then she told Ed to go back to the house and get the ring and mail it to me in New York."

I squeezed his hand; we were nearly back at the restaurant. "I can't believe this."

"Well, believe it. And I'll make sure your life from here on out is a happy one."

We had a fabulous dinner at Tavern on the Green, and a horse and carriage were waiting for us when we walked out, apparently right on Nash's schedule.

Three weeks later, we were wed back in our hometown, so Nash's mom could attend. It was a beautiful day, and she wore a gorgeous, sparkly blue dress and clapped her hands and yelled, "Halleluiah!" when the preacher announced we were man and wife.

For our honeymoon, we spent a week in Bermuda, although we both decided it was a horrible waste of money as we were sure room service would have tasted the same at the L and L back home. It soon became obvious, not only was Nash making up for lost time in the bedroom, he had also been spending a lot of time thinking of creative ways for us to pleasure each other, as we spent every moment in each other's arms.

A friend of Nash's flew us from Cold Springs to Bermuda and back, so we promised Nash's mom a more extended visit on our way back. Thus, it was that we were leaving Pin Oak Manor Retirement Center at seven o'clock in the evening and headed to Nash's mom's place. When Nash nosed his blue truck into the gravel drive our two houses shared he stopped, looking up the slope to the houses.

"Are you sure you're okay with sleeping here? We could head back to the city tonight if you want."

I'll admit, coming back to town made me a nervous wreck at first, but I was determined not to let my past dominate my life.

"No," I said slowly, a chill running up my spine even as I said it. "The sky is looking pretty ominous. And, besides, there are a lot more good memories here," I grabbed his hand and squeezed it, "than bad. And once I get inside your house, any bad memories will be locked out."

But I was wrong about that. When I stepped foot into Nash's kitchen, the only thing I could remember was finding Nash's mom babbling nonsense to me on the day of her first stroke. It was horrifying. I stopped so suddenly Nash almost rammed me with the suitcases as he was coming in behind me.

"Are you okay?"

I tried to leave the uncertainty out of my response. "Yeah...yeah."

But a few hours later, after we spent time cooking our first meal together as man and wife, all ghosts of the past vanished. We were finishing up the dishes when Nash looked at me with a twinkle in his eye, and came over to kiss me. He lifted me up on the counter, then stood massaging my legs.

"You know," he said mischievously, "there is no greater turn-on than to do it in your parent's bed."

"You're insatiable," I returned, kissing him. "And very...very...naughty." I separated my words with kisses and then wrapped my legs tightly around him. He swept me off the counter, his hands under my backside, and took me to the stairs.

Hours later, we were famished again, and came down to raid the fridge. I was wearing an old button-down shirt of Nash's and my panties; he had pulled on a pair of jeans. We found a gallon of ice cream and sat on the kitchen table, knee-to-knee passing the box back and forth, too lazy to bring the chairs back in, which we took out in order to sweep after dinner.

We had barely gotten started when the lights flickered. The rain which threatened all day had let loose in torrents twenty minutes before, and now, it would appear, we would be in for some wicked lightning and thunder.

"I'd better go find a flashlight while I still can," he said begrudgingly. "I think we have a big lantern-type one in the basement." He slipped off the table, pausing before relinquishing the box. "Leave some for me," he warned.

"Of course, sweetheart," I responded innocently.

He was only gone about thirty seconds when the power went out, leaving me in total darkness. I got off the table to try to feel for a dish rag or towel to wipe away some sticky drops of ice cream which fell onto my leg. I leaned against the sink and idly watched the trees swaying out the picture window across from me, illuminated from behind by a streetlight which hadn't been affected by our outage, waiting for Nash. A flash of lightning lit up the silhouette of a figure outside the kitchen door.

"Nash!" I screamed in terror.

"What is it, babe?" he asked, rushing in from the next room with a huge, camping light.

"Someone's outside."

He ran to the door where I pointed and peered through the slanting rain. He clicked on the outdoor light out of habit, receiving no flicker of response, but another burst of lightning illuminated the entire back yard for him. He locked the handle and turned back to me.

"No one's out there," he said gently as he walked back to me.

"I g-guess I'm a bit...jumpy."

He set the lantern on the table and pulled me into his warm arms, where I melted like candle wax on a Chianti bottle. "My god, you're trembling. I should have taken you back home, to New York."

I hugged him tighter. "No, I'm fine. Storms make me jittery, I guess." I remembered it was storming the night I climbed through the window upstairs into Nash's room. I found comfort in his arms that night. "Why don't we sleep in your old room?"

"But a twin mattress is in there."

I looked up at him with a smile. "We won't need much room." I wiggled my eyebrows.

"Oh-ho-ho." He draped his free arm around my shoulder. "Your wish is my command."

I had only begun to contemplate all the possibilities of that statement when a loud crack of thunder made me jump, followed by the distinct sound of breaking glass. We turned in tandem, and, even in the dark, could see the hand reaching through the open pane to grab the door knob. Before we could even react the door opened and a man with a shotgun stepped out of the rain and into the kitchen. Nash brought the light up and I gasped when it revealed the man's face. Nash stepped protectively in front of me.

"What the hell are you doing here, Tate?" Nash growled.

"Now is that any way to greet your father-in-law?" He looked me in the eye as I peered around Nash. "Hey, Chloe-girl." His voice managed to be both velvety and rough.

"Don't talk to her!" Nash screamed, throwing a hand around me.

Tate slowly raised the rifle. "I don't think you quite understand who holds the power here, Nabry." He jerked the barrel to with a loud *click*.

Nash lunged forward with a roar, pushing me down with the hand he had around me. I fell to the floor at a safe distance, but turned, in horror, toward the scuffling. The lantern landed on its side, but luckily, hadn't gone out. It cast crazy shadows as the two men wrestled around on the floor. I fought to determine who was on top, and to my relief, it was Nash. With one more resounding punch, Tate lay still. The lights chose that moment to flicker back to life and he surveyed his victim for a second before turning to me.

"Are you okay?"

"Fine," I answered, rising to my feet. "You?"

"Yeah." With the back of his hand, he wiped a small amount of blood from his mouth. He stood and started to walk toward me, but before he even took his first step, Tate flew up and grabbed him around his legs, sending him crashing to the floor. I screamed, searching the kitchen floor for Tate's shotgun. It lay under the table and I dove for it, but as my fingers touched the cold metal of the barrel, it slid away from me, the sight cutting my finger as it was ripped from my grasp. I looked up as Tate struggled to his feet, the muzzle of the gun now inches from my face. We stared at each other wordlessly. He glanced across the room, keeping the gun pointed at me. I looked in that direction. Nash was coming to his feet across the room. His chin was split open, from where, I presumed, he hit the floor, and he looked a little dazed.

"On your knees, Nabry," Tate ordered sharply, spitting out blood from some internal cut. I looked back at my stepfather. The barrel was close enough for me to grab, but when I glanced up, he was eying me. He moved so quickly, I didn't even see it coming before the tip of the barrel cracked against my cheekbone. "Don't you even think about it." Without saying anything more, he slowly moved the barrel down to my chest, trying to move the fabric of my shirt open with it. He chuckled coarsely, then suddenly swung the gun to point it at Nash, who looked like he had been caught gathering himself to spring. "*I said on your knees!*" Tate hissed between his teeth. Nash complied, looking at me intently, silently apologizing for letting Tate get the best of him. I hoped he could see in my eyes, too, how sorry I was all this was happening.

"Get your hands behind your fucking head!" Tate barked, and slowly Nash raised them, lacing them behind his head and glaring at Tate. I got to my feet, thinking any move I would make would have a better chance if I was more mo-bile. "That's better," Tate said, relaxing a little. He slid his gaze to me for a sec-ond, then back to Nash, speaking to me out of the corner of his mouth. "You try anything, Chloe-girl and I'll put a fucking hole right through your pretty husband's face."

"O-o-okay, Tate," I said shakily, looking at Nash again in fear.

"That's my girl," he said silkily. He ran his gaze over me. "You look *good* girl," he added in a way which had the hairs standing up on my arms. "I'm sure you made a fine bride." His gaze wandered over me again, and I pulled at the hem of my shirt, trying to hide myself. He chuckled at that, and then looked at Nash again. "I'm guessin' my invitation got lost in the mail, huh, Nabry?" he spat. Nash made no reply. Tate looked at me again, tasting me with his eyes, making a decision. "You're gonna come with me, baby."

"The hell she will."

Without warning, Tate swung the gun and cracked Nash across the face with it, sending him sprawling with a loud *THUD*.

"Nash!" I started forward.

"Move again, Chloe and I'll make you a widow." I froze. He turned back and kicked Nash in the ribs with his boot, lifting his body off the floor. Nash groaned loudly, instinctively curling up to try to protect himself.

"Stop! Stop!" I screamed, but Tate wasn't listening.

He turned Nash over easily with the toe of his boot. He still had one arm curled protectively over his ribs, but his near arm flopped to the floor. Then, with some sick war-cry, Tate jumped up in the air and came down on Nash's ex-tended arm. I could hear the bones shatter as Nash cried out in pain, a cry that would haunt my dreams for a lifetime.

Despite what Tate said, I rushed to Nash's side, curling myself around him.

"Please, please," I cried hysterically.

"Get out of the way, Chloe. Or I'll give you some of the same medicine I've given you before."

"Tate," I cried out in desperation. "*Please* don't hurt him anymore." I sobbed. "I'll do anything...*anything* you want."

He considered this. "Then come here," he said, his voice low.

I squeezed Nash, who was moaning beside me, and began to crawl toward Tate, my muscles shaking. When I got within a couple feet he held out his hand to stop me.

"Kneel," he said, his breathing irregular. I could tell he was getting off on this, but I didn't care, as long as he didn't hurt Nash anymore.

"Now..." He licked his lips. "Put your hands behind your head like he did."

Slowly, I raised my hands and laced them behind my head.

He continued to look me over, his eyes blazing. "You know what I want."

I nodded slowly.

"I'm wanting a lot more than a few hours."

I cringed, my stomach falling away, but nodded again.

He stepped up a little, and stuck the cold muzzle of the gun against the skin of my chest again. I flinched, and his mouth spread into a slow grin. He used the gun to pull my shirt out and away from me. He stepped over to look down my shirt, groaning. "Ohh, yess. Pappy's gonna love explorin' his baby's curves." I closed my eyes, disgusted. The barrel moved between my legs and my eyes popped open. He rubbed the barrel back and forth across my pelvis, pushing it up as he did and closed his eyes for a minute with another sick moan. "Uum, yes. I've been waiting to get in between those thighs for a while." His eyes snapped open and they were cold and hard and calculating. My insides turned to ice. Nash shifted behind me, still making low groaning noises. I knew Tate would beat him, even as he raped me, so I began to formulate a plan, hoping against hope Nash could hear me.

"T-tate, we can't do this here." I got to my feet slowly. "Not with my husband lying a few feet away. I know a place. We can get a room," I said distinctly, praying my message was getting through to Nash.

"Ahh. I knew my Chloe-girl had a bit of the nasty in her." He reached over and grabbed me by the back of my hair, squeezing me against him. He pulled my head back and I cried out in pain, but stilled, wanting him to think I was compliant, even willing. He began to kiss my exposed neck and chest. I shivered uncontrollably. "Let's go," he said huskily. He pushed me toward the door and I stumbled a little, but righted myself. I opened the door and looked one more time over at Nash, but he was lying too still, and my heart seized. Maybe he hadn't heard a word and I would be stuck in a hotel room with Tate. What could I do against him alone?

Tate pushed me out in the rain and closed the door behind us.

CHAPTER EIGHTEEN

Nash

My head was throbbing, pulsing like a police cruiser's lights. With an effort, I opened my eyes to the ugly vinyl flooring which had been in our kitchen for over twenty some odd years. What was I doing back here? And did somebody get the license plate number of the truck that hit me? I picked my head up slowly and turned to put it down on the opposite side. The vinyl was cool to this cheek, and comforting. Where was Chloe?

With a suddenness that shook me, my eyes popped open. Chloe. She was here...and then... I urged my addled brain to work. Tate came. I attempted to push myself up to my knees, but fell to one side, a yelp ripped from my throat. A white, blaring pain robbed me of everything else but its presence. My God. What happened to me? I held down, with an effort, the rise of bile in my throat. But even as I did, each beat of my heart seemed to scream "Chloe!" How long was I out? Was I too late to save her?

I staggered to my feet, my arm dangling by my side, and stumbled forward to lean, with my good arm, against the kitchen table, trying to draw my breath. A car started outside. I shoved away from the table and propelled myself to the door, falling against it heavily. Rain slicked the floor, my muddled head noted. I watched the car back down the winding driveway, its lights swinging out to illuminate the front of Chloe's house, and then back to light the area between our two houses. Had it only been a few seconds, then?

I pressed my head against the cold glass above where Tate broke in, trying to clear it, my eyes shut as I focused my thoughts. Chloe was talking to Tate, but she was trying to leave me a message, I was sure of it. And then I remembered.

I yanked the door open and ran through the downpour, slipping and sliding in the mud. Once, I fell on my bad arm. I screamed to the heavens, rolling over on my back in the mud, the rain pounding my chest, synching itself, it seemed, to my heartbeat. I wanted to give up, go to sleep there, in the rain. It seemed almost as comforting as it was hostile. But I couldn't. I needed to help Chloe. "NO!" I yelled into the darkness, breathing heavily. I rolled back over, levering myself up with my one arm to my knees, plopping one foot down in the mud, and straightening my spine little by little until I was upright. I made it to the truck and got in. Thankfully, picking up again on my small town mentality since I'd been home, I'd left my keys in the ignition. I had to reach over myself to close the door. For a minute I wondered why, now that I shut the loudness of the elements out—the wind, the lightning and thunder—why then was it so loud? Then I realized the rain was pounding with such intensity on the rusty roof of the cab, it sounded like tiny Indian tomahawks, or their owners, doing a war dance.

I started the truck and tore off down the driveway, spraying rock and mud everywhere, riding across the lawn in places to save time. When I hit the rural road connected with the drive, I gunned the engine. I could hardly see through the driving rain, but it didn't matter, I knew where I was going. Still, I nearly missed a curve, going across the shoulder and sinking one tire into the ditch on the other side before I could right my truck. I became more mindful.

When I flew into the parking lot of the L and L, my lights swung around capturing first, Chloe running through the rain, and then, Tate taking aim at her with his shotgun. My heart pounding, I mashed the gas pedal to the floor and steered between the two, slamming on the brakes with a screech and coming to a jarring stop. I ducked at the last minute, the report of the rifle thundered and the bullet shattered my passenger-side window. Through a rain of glass I opened my door and screamed for Chloe, but the wind and the rain carried my voice away. I watched her disappear into a tree-line at the far end of the property. Tate cussed and sloshed through the rain. He must be crazy to risk waking people with the sound of his gun, or drunk. I tumbled out of the cab and took off in the direction Chloe had taken, staying as low as I could, leaving the car engine on and the door open, knowing we were abandoning our best escape route.

Another shot pierced the air, and a piece of bark flew from one of the trees ahead of me. When I hit the woods, I veered at a diagonal, hoping to throw Tate off. I wanted to call for Chloe, but knew, even if she could hear me, which I doubted, I may be making it easier for Tate to hone in on us. Then, with the flash of lightning overhead, I spotted her. She leaned her back against a tree, gasping for breath, but branches broke somewhere to our right, in between us. I needed to circle around to the left and get to her before Tate did.

I lost sight of her in the dense foliage at one point, but when I broke through again, I was behind her. She must have heard Tate, because she had stepped away from the tree, with one hand still on its trunk, trying to peer around from the protection of its wide base. I snuck up and clapped my hand over her mouth.

In terror, she screamed and bit down on my flesh, easily breaking free, since I had no arm to hold her with.

"Chloe," I whispered hoarsely.

She swung around, peering through the rain. I breathed a sigh of relief when she ran and threw her arms around me. It sent a fire raging through my arm, but I didn't care. I clasped her to me with my good arm and her mouth found mine, incredibly warm even as the cold rain continued to wash over us. As foolish as it was, we continued to kiss, the rain seeping in between our mouths at times in a way which would have been incredibly arousing if we weren't being chased by a mad man, and if Chloe weren't squeezing my mangled arm, and my hand wasn't burning where she bit me.

I grunted. "Umm. If your stepfather doesn't finish me off, I think you will, hon.'"

"Oh. Your arm. I'm sorry. I'm sorry about *all* of this." I could tell she was stricken with guilt.

"You are not responsible for what that son of a bitch of a stepfather does."

"I know, but—"

I put a finger to her lips to still her, having heard something uphill.

"Chloe, dammit! When I catch you, it'll be the last beating you'll ever get from me. Because I won't stop until your blood runs cold through my fingers."

Her face became ashen and she swayed. I knew she was petrified. I gave her shoulder a squeeze with my good hand and motioned for her to follow me downhill. It quickly became apparent we were headed toward water as, even over the rain splattering on the tree leaves, came the thunder of a stream.

In seconds we emerged on its muddy banks. It was probably one of those creeks which ran dry during droughts, but tonight it was a torrent, swelling high up its banks and hurtling debris downstream. We moved along the water, trying to stay behind the cover of the trees. Chloe was in front; I was trying to keep myself between her and Tate, but all of a sudden she gave a short scream which was cut off abruptly.

I turned back and Chloe was rolling down the slope of the creek bed, looking like a child playing as they tumbled down a grassy hill. Only this hill wasn't grassy, it was made of mud and rock. With all the rain, the path we were traveling eroded out from under her and sent her twisting down. Her head bounced off one of the bigger rocks right before she hit the water with a splash. She disappeared under the surface.

In a panic, I scrambled down the side of the hill, trying to keep an eye on the spot where she vanished. I started sliding, and fell on my side, but managed to keep from squashing my injured arm under me. When I reached the creek, I waded in. The water was deep, and churning as it cascaded down the hillside. I had to be careful to balance my weight and keep my footing to avoid being swept along. I felt along the bottom for Chloe, but finally immersed myself, searching with my hands along the bed of the creek. I began to wonder if she hadn't sunk at all, but was carried downstream instead. I came up for air, and dove back in, moving a little downstream as I did. Finally, when I thought my lungs would collapse, my hand brushed against the sleeve of my shirt, the one Chloe was wearing, but I had to come up. My head cleared the top of the water and I gasped for air, taking it in with large gulps. How long had she been under water? It seemed like an eternity, but maybe it was only minutes. And how would I pull her out with only one arm?

I dove again and tried to tug on her, finally getting parallel enough to the creek bed that I could sort of wedge my shoulders under hers and get her up enough to throw my good arm over her. Even so, I was surprised by how difficult it was to lift her, as weighed down as she was by water. Not to mention how encumbered I was by my disabled left arm. I made an attempt to kick off the bottom, but holding my breath for so long and struggling against the water made me dizzy and weak. With one final surge, I broke the surface and was able to drag her up, too. Through a combination of pushing off the bottom and straining my body forward, we made some progress toward the bank, although between each effort we moved further downstream. After several minutes I reached the bank and pulled her up alongside me. I melted into the mud, exhausted, staring into her pale face. A gash was opened above her right eye and the area had swelled considerably. Had I rescued my wife's corpse?

"Don't move, Nabry." He was above us. But I wasn't even sure if I *could* move, both arms lying lifelessly beside me, half-in and half-out of the water. I strained to lift my head. Tate stood on the bank, the moon shining down behind him like some sort of mixed-up halo. I flexed my fingers, thinking of using them to push up. I wasn't about to die lying down. He would have to shoot the legs out from under me. But my fingers scraped against something cold and sharp.

"Thought you could take her from me, huh?" His voice carried to me between thunder claps. "Thought I was some stupid old man who would roll over and play dead. Thought—"

I lobbed the rock, but he saw it coming somehow. He ducked, but lost his balance. Pitching forward, he dropped the gun, which skittered down within inches of me. He went careening over the edge with a splash. Flailing around, he screamed, "Save me! I can't swim!"

I looked at him, incredulous, and a rush of water took him under. I waited, expecting him to emerge again further downstream, but there was no other sign of him. Could I let the man die in front of me? Part of me raged—he deserved it. Part of me knew I would be haunted by it if I did. I plunged into the water, letting the current carry me downstream to about the spot he went under. Luckily, the area was fairly well lit by some business's parking lot's lights on the other side of the stream, shining through the sparser foliage on that side. I dove under and felt around, half afraid his hand would grab me and keep me under to die with him. When I came up for air, I glanced in Chloe's direction and the current was about to take her out again, the only thing keeping her ashore was the sucking quality of the mud.

Now what? If I dove for Tate again, she might get carried off right over my head and end up drowning. I judged I probably had one more dive left before she was freed from the side and quickly submerged myself. I searched frantically, but only found more rock. Something bumped into me and I climbed back to the surface. I broke the water barely in time to snag the collar of Chloe's shirt as she sped past me. Even so, she almost slid right out of the over-sized shirt and followed the current. I tugged on the collar, managing to get her to the side again. My tired muscles screamed, and I coughed up the dirty creek water which had splashed in while I took a breath.

The next thing I remember was waking up on a stretcher in the middle of the L and L parking lot.

They were getting ready to lift me into the back of an ambulance. I recognized the EMT as someone I went to school with, Josh McDaniels. "Chloe?" My voice was raspy.

"She already left in another ambulance," a voice answered me from the right. I moved my head slowly to find the speaker. Even dripping wet I recognized Ralph Denegan. The mechanic nodded at me when our eyes met, as if to reassure me. Did he think I didn't know what he had done to Chloe?

"What is *he* doing here?" I said to no one in particular.

"Nash," Josh admonished. "It was Ralph who called us. By the time we got here he had Chloe up to the parking lot and he led us right to you."

Ralph shrugged. "I heard that crazy old bastard out here shootin' off his gun like it was the friggin' Fourth of July, so I followed him. Saw him do his final belly flop, too. Gave it a 9.5," he drawled complacently.

"You should have jumped in after him. You two were cut from the same cloth."

"Now, I never laid a hand on Chloe. Well, never hurt her, anyways."

Josh looked from me to Ralph and back curiously.

"Do you really think so?"

The mechanic looked down and shuffled his feet in the loose gravel, his hands stuck in his pockets. He raised his head and peered at me, his face still with the same blank look. "You might be right about that," he said simply, then turned and walked back to one of the rooms. A young girl stood in the doorway waiting for him. She reached up and locked her arms around his neck, kissing him and pulling him into the room. He turned as he closed the door and our gazes locked. He paused for a second, but then finished closing the door with a soft click. As much as a parasite as I thought he was, he looked so pathetic, I almost had to feel sorry for him. Then I thought about the fact he had been alone with an unconscious Chloe, and that made me cringe.

I decided right then it was okay for me to hate his guts.

Chloe

It was dark when I woke. I looked around uncertainly. I was in a hospital room, that much was clear. The attempt which had been made to make the place homey was depressing. Dark green floral curtains hung over the windows and a mismatched white, flowered wallpaper border created a chair-rail around the room, separating a mint green from a forest green like a referee separating opponents in a hockey fight. My head was groggy and unfocused, and a dull pain over my right eye reminded me why I came. It was raining, and slick, and I lost my footing and slid down a creek bank and bumped my head on a rock. But why was I messing around by the creek in the rain?

Then, like the lightning bolt which outlined him in the doorway of Nash's house, I remembered seeing Tate. And remembered him hurting Nash. In a panic I turned my head too quickly to search for my newlywed husband, but a wave of nausea made me close my eyes. I waited for my brain to catch up to the motion of my head, like the ping-pong lottery balls coming bouncing to a stop. I waited with baited breath to open my eyes. A soft, rhythmic noise thrummed nearby and I slowly opened my eyes to identify it.

And there was Nash, asleep, with his head bent back over the top of a chair, his neck at a crazy angle. His feet were up on a second chair he had pulled over, one stuck through the gap between the back of the chair and the seat, one bent. His big, size eleven shoe, muddied beyond description, posed perilously on the edge of the chair. One arm was looped over the back of the chair he was sitting on, one in a sling. His hair was a total mess, smashed flat against his head on one side, sticking out everywhere on the other. He had on scrubs, and his mouth hung open as he snored.

And he was the most precious sight in the world. My heart swelled with love for him. *What a goof. But he's my goof. And he's safe.*

He looked pretty good, some bruising on the left side of his face, and his chin was bandaged, but all and all, he looked really good.

He came. He understood I was going to have Tate take me to the L and L and he showed up in time. I flashed back to the image of him kneeling on the floor with his hands behind his head. I was so terrified of what Tate would do to him, but here he sat, rumpled and disheveled, with a few cuts and bruises, but he was okay. Tears of relief welled up in my eyes as I watched him sleep, deliriously happy to be in the same room with him.

"Well. Look who's up?" a nurse said cheerily as she walked in the door. I held a finger to my lips and she walked over, exaggeratedly, on tiptoes so as not to wake Nash. She had to be the one who decorated the room, I decided. She had wild, curly red-orange hair and an outrageously chipper personality. But when she noticed the tears in my eyes, she became concerned. "Oh, dear. Are you in pain?"

"No. No. I'm fine."

She patted my hand. "You've been through a lot, sugar. It's okay if you want to cry."

We both jumped at the loud clanging caused by Nash's feet getting caught in his chair as he stood. He rushed to my side. "Chloe. Are you okay?"

"I'm fine," I repeated, ruffling his hair with a smile as he bent over me.

"Thank God," he said with a sigh which turned to a smile. His face turned serious again. "I won't let him hurt you ever again." He brushed my hair back from a bandage I now felt on my head, and kissed me. He laid his forehead on mine. "Never Chloe. I promise."

"I know."

"I'll give you kids a few minutes," the nurse said tactfully, and exited.

No sooner had she left, when Ed stuck his head in the door. "Heeyy, Little Bits. Glad to see you up." He came over to the bed and laid one of his massive hands on my leg. "How ya feelin'?"

"Like I have a hangover. Minus the fun of the night before."

Ed laughed long and hard. "Well, that sucks. Really," he said, taking my hand with surprising gentleness. "I'm glad you're okay."

I blinked back tears, swallowing the lump in my throat. "Thanks, Ed."

"Now." His voice boomed. He wrapped his arm around Nash's neck and rubbed his scalp viciously with the knuckles of his other hand. "Mind if I borrow this chucklehead for a minute?"

I laughed. "No, go ahead."

He took Nash out into the hall but Ed's idea of a whisper was everyone else's idea of a shout. "I didn't want to tell you in front of Chloe..." I was surprised to hear him use my name. Up until that point I wasn't even sure he knew it. "...but the body of Tate Rodgers was found washed up down in Broome County."

I couldn't hear Nash's response, but Ed picked up again. "Yeah. You *could* have saved him and lost your wife. If you're feeling guilty about not saving that bastard's sorry ass, I'm gonna have the doctor check that head of yours again. That man tried to kill you and Chloe. It could have as easily been one of you two washing up two counties from here, you know? Or maybe you liked staring down the barrel of that man's shotgun and having him ogle your wife like some kind of leech?"

This time I could hear Nash's answer because he raised his voice in anger. "Shut up! You know I didn't like the way he treated her!"

"Then don't feel guilty about his death. You didn't kill him, dammit. And—" his voice became softer. "I'm sorry for yelling at you. It's just...I don't much like the idea of attending my little brother's funeral."

They continued talking, but I tuned them out. Tate was dead. I tried the words out in my brain to see how I felt about it. I received no response. No sorrow, no guilt, no anything. Nash came back in, looking pale and wiping his hands on his pant leg. My gaze flickered to his anxiously. Reading my face, he approached my bedside slowly.

He took my hand. "Babe...I've got something to tell you." He looked at my hand, brushing his thumb across it. "You probably don't remember much about what happened last night," he began carefully.

Last night? Had it been that long? Was it morning?

"—but, the path we were walking on eroded out from under your feet and you rolled down the bank and hit your head on a rock before splashing into the creek." I nodded. "I pulled you out, but then Tate was on the top of the bank and pointing his gun at us. I lobbed a rock at him, and he ducked. But he lost his footing and ended up in the water, too." He paused, his face scrunching up. "He couldn't swim and he went under. I tried to get to him, but then you floated free again and I had to pull you back to the bank, and...I think I passed out after that." He looked up into my eyes. "Tate is dead, honey. They found his body downstream. I'm sorry."

I nodded. And then the tears started coming.

"Oh, honey." He hugged me, though hindered by the bedrail, my IV, and his cast arm. "I'm so sorry. I did the best I could, I swear."

"No, Nash. It's not that."

He searched my eyes. "Then what is it?"

"It's...I feel...nothing. Absolutely nothing." I raised my arms, palm up. "Shouldn't I feel something?"

"Oh...well." He cleared his throat. "Maybe it's going to take a while to sink in."

I shook my head. "I know he's dead. I guess I don't care. What kind of a daughter am I?"

"Oh, don't question that, Chloe. You were the best daughter in the world to your dad, and he loved you more than anything. Tate was no father to you. He was mean, and abusive. He—"

"I know, but he was a man. Shouldn't I feel something?"

"I don't know." His brow furrowed. "You can only feel what you feel, Clo."

"Yeah, but I should feel something."

"Don't you feel anything? Anything at all?"

I shrugged. "Relief? Isn't that awful?"

"No."

We were interrupted by the arrival of the doctor.

The next morning, after I was released from the hospital, we returned to New York City. Nash drove straight to the warehouse, insisting on driving despite the cast on his arm.

"You're putting me to work already?" I complained.

"Nope," he returned, shutting off the engine. "No more work for you here."

"What? No, come on. I was kidding." I continued to protest as he walked around and opened my door.

"Nuh-uh-uh. Not another word. We're not here to work. We're here so I can carry you over the threshold of our new home."

"Oh, Nash," I practically squealed. "That sounds so nice."

"Yes, it does."

"But, your arm."

He lifted me with his good arm so suddenly I screamed. I hung on tightly to him, trying to take the weight from him. Happiness bubbled up inside me. I was so thankful we had found our way back to each other despite everything that happened to us. He carried me to the building and struggled to get the door open, but finally stepped inside. He turned to a newly installed bank of switches, bringing the room to life one corner at a time. I gasped. All of the plans we talked about together spread out before me like magic. A large fountain in the middle, with its welcome, soothing noise, cozy sitting areas spread throughout, and, everywhere, his beautiful artwork displayed on walls of varied designs, to enhance their natural allure. He had the floors done while we were in Bermuda and they shone to a high gloss, and the track lighting was well-thought-out, illuminating everything with a soft light.

"It's beautiful," I cried, my eyes wide, trying to take it all in. He set me down lightly, admiring it for the first time himself.

"Man, it turned out nice." We stepped in further, but before I could do any more exploring, he grabbed my hand. "Upstairs." He ran to the staircase, racing up and dragging me behind him.

"You had the furniture brought over." The kitchen was finished when we left, but none of the furniture was moved in.

"Ed and Ronnie did it for us. It was their wedding present."

"It looks perfect," I gushed. "Sissy and Emily must have helped."

"No doubt. Ed and Ronnie's idea of home décor is a beer can pyramid."

The room was now a great room, a spacious kitchen on the far right, with a half-wall bar on the rear side of the apartment separating it from a dining room with a long table which served at least ten. The kitchen and dining room were one step up from the living room we stood in, and someone managed to find a couch which was an exact match for mine so there were two couches and several large chairs in the middle with an over-sized square ottoman which also served as a coffee-table. A fireplace, open on all four sides, stood between the living room and kitchen. The whole place had a homey feel. I could already see Ed and Ronnie slouched on the couch, watching a Rangers game with Nash, while Sissy and Emily sat at the bar chatting with me as I put the finishing touches on appetizers for us all. In a word, it was home.

"Come on." He tugged on my hand again. "One last surprise."

He opened the door to his bedroom, *our* bedroom, and let me pass through. I entered and then stood stock still, staring. The light from the two large windows we had put in right before the wedding cast a friendly glow on the interior of the room. Although the gigantic, beautiful honeyed-oak, four-poster bed was unexpected, the biggest shock was what hung over the bed.

"B-but how...?"

Nash smiled, seeming to take delight in surprising me. "I offered them a copy, and promised to paint four more, in addition to this one."

Above our bed hung the Imagine painting. It made this place our own special oasis, reminding me again of the tree house.

"Oh, Nash!" My hand flew over my mouth as the tears began to roll down my face. Painted in the bottom right-hand corner were the words, "From the beginning and from this day forward, I will love you, forever. –Nash," and next to it, the date of our wedding. I turned to look at him—my friend, my lover, my cohort in crime. My head spun with the realization all the heartache which followed us from Cold Springs was now behind us and our future spread out before us here in the home we created together.

And I couldn't imagine anything sweeter.

"Welcome home, Chloe Marie Nabry. Welcome home." His arms slid around me, one in a plaster cast, the other, as solid and reassuring, and I knew nothing would ever separate us again.

Note from author

Thank you for reading HOMETOWN HEARTACHE, part of my REAL ROMANCE COLLECTION. I hope you enjoyed it. Now that you've read the book, won't you please consider writing a review? Reviews are one of the best ways readers discover great new books. They don't need to be fancy or long, just a sentence or two honestly describing your opinion of/experience with the book. I would sincerely appreciate it.

Want more from M.J. Schiller?

Page forward for

an excerpt from

TAKE A CHANCE ON ME

Book Six in the REAL ROMANCE
COLLECTION

TAKE A CHANCE ON ME

Five-Foot-Two-Eyes-Of-Blue. That's what he'd been calling her for weeks. Cash Delmonaco slid into the end seat at a blackjack table, where he could keep an eye on the suspect, although that wasn't where his gaze was focused at the moment. He watched her hands—beautiful, graceful—as the cards arced like a rainbow between them. They slapped onto the table, one at a time, intermixing like couples at a speed dating event, the noise satisfyingly sharp. Like his nerves. And not because he was investigating a "probable" prostitution ring with "possible" mob tie-ins that was "likely" laundering money. Yeah, Victory, New York might not be Vegas, but vice wasn't picky about locations. Vice went where the action was. Where the money was. But he'd be damned if that happened on his watch. He wanted, *needed* to keep this town clean. In memory of his parents.

But all that aside, his pulse wasn't racing because he was some action junkie cop. His adrenaline was fueled by what would affect any red-blooded male. Her. He lifted his head, his gaze traveling over delicate wrists, up her arms, and across the swell of her breasts. Her chest was draped in black silk, the skin hidden from view, although the way she filled the material tantalized him. She had a perfect column of a neck. He paused, imagining his lips brushing along the hollow there. After a few seconds, his view continued to climb. An appealing full mouth, flawlessly shaped. China-doll skin, and—BAM!—those eyes. Bluer than the waters of the Greek isles, which he'd only seen in pictures.

She must have felt him looking at her because she raised her head and their gazes connected. His smile was automatic, involuntary. She drew in a breath and her hands faltered, a card squirting out of the pack, soaring halfway across the table. She snatched it off the green felt, sliding it back into the fold while peeking over her shoulder. The move didn't escape her pit boss's attention and the large Asian man raised his eyebrows, arms crossed, frowning at her.

"Sorry," she said demurely without looking up. "It won't happen again."

He growled but moved on to the next table.

She rolled a shoulder as if pushing back the chill of his disapproval and gave herself a slight shake, suddenly nothing but business. "All bets down?" She skimmed her painted fingernails over the table, checking that everyone had their chips in place, then dealt.

Her table was always full. And it was no wonder. The ultimate combination of girl-next-door and sex kitten. Who wouldn't want to take cards from her? Even when the cards were as weak as a nine and a three, when the dealer showed a two, which was the case at the moment. He knew a player was always supposed to assume the dealer's under card was a ten, as it had the highest chances to be a ten, with all the face cards equaling that value. That would mean, if he stayed with his twelve, he would at least bump, and not lose any money. And if he took a card, he would likely end up with a ten, giving him twenty-two, and he would bust, losing the hand. But there were also a whole lot of combinations she could have that would beat his twelve....

He felt Ian behind him rather than saw him. The result of partnering for so long.

"You've got to hit on that," he whispered.

"Shut up."

She'd finished with the other players, who all seemed to have good cards. He was up.

Throwing a look over her shoulder again, she leaned in, close enough he could catch her scent. Apple pie and leather. The paradox fit.

"Your friend's right," she murmured.

He raised his head. Her eyes showed laughter.

If he tipped his chin and moved an inch, those lips would be his. Not the best move, though. Might seem a bit forward, seeing as they'd never met.

Ian bent to speak into his ear, his gaze on the dealer. "I've heard it said you're more likely to lose your heart at La Bonne Chance than your money. After tonight, I'd have to say they're right. A lot of these dealers are lookers."

But there's only one I'm looking at.

But why's he looking at her?

His partner, though married now, had been a ladies' man in his day, and if he'd do anything, Cash would keep him away from this dealer. He swiveled in his chair and glared at his friend.

Ian held up his hands. "Okay. Okay." He walked away.

With a sigh, Cash gestured for another card, and she flipped it over. A nine. Twenty-one. Things were looking up. She smiled and nodded. Dimples, too. He was a goner.

She turned over a five and dealt herself an eight. *Bust.* Everyone cheered, and she paid up. He put down a two-chip tip for her and checked on the suspect.

The huge African-American guy looked like he was stuffed into his impeccable black suit. His electric blue tie, perfectly knotted, must be special ordered to fit his tree trunk neck. *Why is everyone a behemoth in here?* Cash had passed him earlier and noted a flat nose that he always seemed to be looking down, and small, close-set eyes. A gold nametag read Lewis DePesto, Floor Supervisor, Detroit, Michigan.

The big man pulled out a chair at the bar for a slender woman whose jet-black hair was drawn up in a sleek bun. Sparkling jewelry dripped from her ears and neck. Her almond eyes were outlined expertly, with that whole smoky thing going on, which he found so appealing. The Lewis guy had one hand on her chair and the other on the back of the adjacent seat, whose occupant turned toward the woman. The guy next to her possessed all the parts to be attractive, he guessed—dark thick hair, white smile, yada yada—but the pieces weren't meshing as they should. He was off. Geeky looking instead of slick. He dressed expensively, but not well, unable to pull the clothes together either. She was *way* out of his league.

"Sir? Do you want to hit?"

"What?" He swiveled back and glanced at his cards. A four and a jack. Fourteen. "Yeah, hit me."

She hesitated long enough for him to know he'd made the wrong play. He looked at her hand. She showed a six. Odds said she would bust.

"I'm sorry. I didn't quite hear you above that lady celebrating her jackpot at the slots." A fifty-some-year-old with bottled red hair screamed and jumped up and down like a lunatic. "I need you to give a clear gesture for the cameras."

He waved another card off, flashing her a smile of gratitude for the second chance, then turned his attention back to the bar. The couple was gone. His heart rate picked up. He searched the floor and spotted her red dress as they slipped into an elevator.

Ian flew in from out of nowhere and stuck his hand between the closing doors to join them. *Covering my ass again. I'll have to buy him a brew for that one.*

"Sir, are you in?"

He moved a couple of chips into the circle on the table across from his chair, and she dealt. He slid his gaze to the bar again. Something had caught his attention earlier. A tall blonde with an up-do similar to the other woman's. She wore an electric blue curve-hugging dress in the same style as the first woman's.

"Do you want a card?"

Her voice had an edge.

"Hmm... Yeah, yeah. I'll take a card." This time he remembered to gesture, tapping the table. He was vaguely aware of the groan from the other players a second or two later. Five-Foot-Two—*I need to quit calling her that. Even if it is only in my head*—raked in his chips. No big deal. His captain had supplied him with gambling money. He'd put in his own if necessary. He glanced at her nametag.

Harper from St. Louis, Missouri. *Well, Harper from St. Louis, I'd love to find out more about you than just your name and state of origin.*

She didn't seem to be aware of his ogling, as she was busy laying out the cards. That red hair of hers, shimmering in the casino's lights, was enough to force the lust to rush through his veins. Remembering he was supposed to be working, he tore his gaze from her and studied the girl in blue again.

The jewelry matches, too.

His gaze roamed.

And my guy Lewis is leading some schmuck there. This one's practically bald and twice her age. Could they be any less subtle?

Minutes later, they rose and headed for the elevators like the other pair. Either these guys were getting incredibly lucky—which he doubted—or money was exchanging hands.

He realized everyone at the table was staring at him. His play. He gestured, and her card flipped before she again took his money.

Or maybe that bartender's serving one mean love potion. I could use some of that for Five-Foot-Two.

Harper! The girl has a name.

The only people at the bar now were a group of guys doing shots. He scanned the area for his suspect and caught him near the elevators, standing with his feet wide, shoulders back, one hand circling the wrist of his other, both resting on his stomach. His gaze skipped about the room, and Cash had to look away when it neared him.

"Insurance?"

A glance back at the table told him Harper had an ace. Thinking insurance was a chump's bet, he declined, as did everyone else at the table. The other card turned out to be the jack of spades. A true blackjack.

Swell.

As she dealt the next hand, a woman approached Lewis. She wore her blonde hair down, straight, and a red halter style dress caressed her body. No jewelry. They talked, looked toward the bar, and she nodded and moved in that direction.

Cash checked his cards. He had eighteen. Good hand this time. Maybe he'd win some back.

Eying the bar again, he noticed the "lady in red's" legs were crossed, the top one bouncing up and down like a Superball. A girly martini sat in front of her as she leaned on the bar with her elbows, staring off into space. She sat on the opposite side of the square bar from the pack of guys, but they zeroed in on her. One straightened his shirt and took a few steps in her direction, but two of his friends grabbed his arms and dragged him back and they all had a good laugh about it.

Murmurs and the scuffling of chairs moving alerted him. She had a friggin' pair of kings. No way.

"Sorry, guys. Enjoy the rest of your time at La Bonne Chance. And come back and see us again."

As his friends discussed their next move, one of the players leaving separated from the herd. Leaning forward, he rested an arm on the table. "What time do you get off, Harper?"

Her eyes widened. "Umm...I'm not sure."

He frowned. "Not sure what time you get off?"

Cash followed the conversation while trying to appear as though he wasn't. The guy looked like the putz at the bar earlier, only his pieces were coming together just fine. Cash gritted his teeth.

"Well...I'm scheduled off at ten, but sometimes they make me stay later. I get a break at nine, though."

"Then why don't you join me for a drink during your break?"

"Uhh...we're not allowed to drink on the clock. And the break's too short anyway."

"Then how about I wait for you until ten over at that bar?" He tilted his head in its direction and swept an arm toward it, too.

What is this jackass doing? She's not interested in him.

Harper hesitated, biting her bottom lip.

Is she?

"We're not supposed to...fraternize with the clientele, sir."

"You can call me Jim. And we're not fraternizing." He glanced at the pit boss, closing the gap between Harper and him even more. "I'm just going to buy a pretty lady a drink, on her own time. What can they say to that?"

Cash stopped breathing, leaning forward a fraction to catch her answer.

The pit boss circled around behind her like a shark in a tank, before stopping to loom over her. She scrambled to deal a hand to Cash and an old drunk at the other end of the table who looked like he was napping.

"I can't," she whispered hoarsely.

Her Don Juan, safe behind the comfort of the table, looked at the boss boldly. Like he could take the three hundred-fifty pounder. He'd be killed. "I'll be right over there, angel." With one last glare at the big man, he threw her a wink and headed off. A false show of bravado, or stupidity? It was hard to say.

Harper exhaled as he walked away and suddenly seemed a whole lot smaller. And vulnerable.

Cash's gaze drifted to the boss, then back to her.

"So, Harper from St. Louis, how long have you worked here?"

"A couple of months." She smiled. "Does it show?"

"No, no. You're doing a great job. A real pro."

She won again.

Crap.

He sucked in a breath through his teeth. "Maybe too good."

Movement in his peripheral vision alerted him. The blonde was up and moving.

"You'd lose less if you weren't so busy looking at her."

He swiveled back to Harper. "Oh, no. Her? No. I just—"

"Save your breath." She shifted and looked beyond him. "She *is* gorgeous." She was flushed and her jaw was tight. Did having Jim wait for her upset her?

She turned to stare at the older guy on the stool for a beat. A soft snore is-sued from his mouth. She shook her head with a small smile and dealt to Cash, leaving the old man's spot empty.

I should get up and move to a busier table where I have more time to scope out the scene without getting caught.

He looked at her again. She pushed a strand of hair behind her ear. Damn. Even her ears were cute. His heart went into rocket mode. He wasn't going any-where.

She reached the white card one of the players stuck in the deck that told her it was time to shuffle. It was that Jim prick who put it there. *What? Was he taking it as foreplay when she asked him to cut the deck? She'd probably asked a zil-lion guys to cut it before, including the snorer.* As she removed the cards from the shoe in order to shuffle, he checked to see if ol' Jimbo was really at the bar.

Yup. Loser.

Harper cleared her throat. "So you know my name. What's yours?"

She looked at the cards.

"Cash."

"Cash," she sputtered, stopping mid-shuffle. "If you were giving me a fake name, at least you could come up with something more original than that." She shook her head. "Cash. The Card Player."

He laughed. "No. I swear. My mama was a huge Johnny Cash fan. Sang me 'Folsom Prison Blues' as a lullaby."

"Nothing like shooting a man to watch him die to put a baby to sleep."

He laughed. He liked her quick wit and the twinkle of fun that never seemed to leave her eye.

"Your mama had good taste though. That's an awesome song."

"It is. One of my favorites. Behind 'Sweet Child of Mine.'"

She looked him straight in the eye. "I love that song." She had a habit of en-gaging with him, then glancing away. Perhaps to avoid *fraternizing.* "And you know, I shouldn't tease about the name. My mom was a huge reader. Guess what my last name is."

Harper...what was the name of that chick who wrote To Kill a Mockingbird? "Lee."

"Nope. Good guess, though. Mine's worse. Harper Collins."

It took him a second. "Like the publisher?"

She nodded.

"Man!"

She laughed. "I told you."

Cash took a drink of his Captain and Coke, which he'd forgotten he even had. She was doing a thorough job of shuffling. Something his aunt would have irritably called, in her deep smoker's voice, "Shuffling the face off the cards." Maybe his sweet little dealer didn't want the conversation to end either. He played with his chips as he studied her, picking them up, then letting them drop, enjoying the clinking sound. He straightened the increasingly short pile before lifting a few again.

"So what brought you all the way from St. Louis to the blustery North?"

She tipped her head to the side and laid out his cards. "A mistake. Would you like a card, Cash?"

Her demeanor had changed again. Shoulders slumped, spark gone out of her eyes. *A mistake?* He chewed on that for a while. *What kind of mistake?* The shadow of her boss darkened the table, and he hurried to signal for a card and busted. She ended up with a soft seventeen. If he'd stayed, she would have most likely busted, or at least he would have bumped and kept his money.

"Sorry."

He grinned. "Yeah. Sure you are."

The smile was back, though weaker. The man at the other end of the table made a particularly loud snore and woke himself with a shake.

"What? Hmm?" He blinked.

She put a hand on his arm. "Hey, Joe. Maybe it's time to go home to Martha."

He rubbed a hand over his face. "Yeah. You're probably right. Thanks, Harper." He collected himself, taking several seconds to come to a full standing position, like his spine was made out of Jell-O.

"You're catching a cab?" Her voice was soft whenever she spoke to him.

"Oh, yeah. You know me. Smart about DUIs. Dumb about cards."

"Oh, no. You know your cards, all right." She nodded sharply. "Lady Luck just wasn't with you tonight."

He looked at Cash, the corners of his lips lifting. "Well, Lady Luck is a—and excuse me for saying this young lady—bitch!" He winked.

Cash chuckled. "She definitely can be." He could tell the kindly older man was somewhat of a character.

"Well," Joe shuffled forward, "I hope you have better luck tonight." He tipped his head toward Harper and put a hand on Cash's arm, turning sideways and leaning in. "Take care of this pretty little lady."

Cash jerked. Was he that obvious? "I'll do what I can," he whispered back.

Joe laughed until he wheezed. "Oh, I'm sure you will."

"Hey. What's with all the whispering?" Harper interjected.

The old man shuffled off, throwing a "Never you mind," over his shoulder and still chuckling. "That's between me and Cash."

He knows my name? Old codger's not as out of it as he seems to be.

Harper frowned. "What did he say?" She was more animated now.

Cash put up a hand. "You heard Joe. It's between him and me."

She watched the old man retreat over his shoulder. "Oh," she huffed. "Whatever. Ante up."

He put his bet in and threw a glance at the bar, almost out of reflex now. Jim was still there, but the blonde joined him. She had a martini on the bar in front of her, as well as an empty glass. She looked a lot...peppier. Jim bent to say something in her ear and she laughed, putting a hand on his shoulder. He drew back, but only a little. He had an elbow on the bar and moved a hand to her knee, stroking her, but casting a look in Harper's direction at the same time. He seemed torn.

Cash returned his concentration to his hand and, having nineteen, upped his bet. She drew a twenty and he reached for his chips for the next round, only to find he was out of them. He dug into his pocket for his wallet. Time for him to play on his own dime. He laid a fifty-dollar bill on the felt, and she converted it to chips, her hands doing the choreographed dance all dealers did. Stacking his chips, measuring them against the next pile, and pouring them out on the table. Finally, she put his bill in the slot near her and pushed it down with the paddle.

A half hour and thirty dollars later, she seemed to sense the new dealer behind her like she had Ian. Nine o'clock. Time for her break. She tipped her head, turning her palms up for the cameras. Cash checked out the couple at the bar. When he turned back, Harper shook her head. "Maybe you should just ask her out."

Cash leaned forward, trying to give her his most charming smile. "Maybe it's not her I want to ask out."

She blinked and seemed about to say something when the pit boss hovered. She looked down. "It was nice meeting you, Cash."

He took his chips and scrambled to his feet. "Time for your break?"

She checked over his shoulder. "I'm off now. I lied to that Jim guy to get him out of my hair. I'm going to try to duck out without him seeing me." She gave him a smile. "Hope your luck turns. Have a good night." The pit boss grabbed her elbow as she turned to leave. "You're not here to flirt."

She snatched her arm back, rubbing it. "I understand that." Her tone was defensive, but she dropped her chin and scurried off. Cash hoped he didn't get her in trouble.

"Are you in, sir?" The new dealer smiled at him.

He watched Harper weave through the crowd to an unmarked door. "No. I'm sitting this one out."

ALSO FROM M.J. SCHILLER

ROMANTIC REALMS COLLECTION:
TAKEN BY STORM
AN UNCOMMON LOVE
LEAP INTO THE KNIGHT
LADY OF THE KNIGHT
A KNIGHT TO REMEMBER

ROCKING ROMANCE COLLECTION:
TRAPPED UNDER ICE
ABANDON ALL HOPE
BETWEEN ROCK AND A HARD PLACE
ROCK ME, GENTLY
MIDNIGHT MELODY

LOVE AND CHAOS SERIES:
ROCKED BY GRACE
ROCKED BY LOVE
ROCK IT TO THE MOON
ROCK OF SALVATION (Coming soon!)

REAL ROMANCE COLLECTION:
UPON A MIDNIGHT CLEAR
THE HEART TEACHES BEST
DAMAGE DONE
BLACKOUT
HOMETOWN HEARTACHE
TAKE A CHANCE ON ME

DEVILISH DIVAS SERIES:

TO HELL IN A COACH BAG
DAMNED IF I DO
THE DEVIL YOU KNOW
SATAN, LINE ONE
PITCHFORK IN THE ROAD
SIN WORTH THE PENANCE
HELL HATH NO FURY

ABOUT THE AUTHOR

Bestselling author M.J. Schiller is a retired lunch lady/romance-romantic suspense writer. She enjoys writing novels whose characters include rock stars, desert princes, teachers, futuristic Knights, construction workers, cops, and a wide variety of others. In her mind everybody has a romance. She is the mother of a twenty-seven-year-old and three twenty-five-year-olds. That's right, triplets! So having recently taught four children to drive, she likes to escape from life on occasion by pretending to be a rock star at karaoke. However...you won't be seeing her name on any record labels soon.